A Novel

ROOTED IN LIES

KASIA CHOJECKI

© Kasia Chojecki

ISBN: 9798540324342
Imprint: Independently published
Cover Image by Kasia Chojecki

To: Maciej (Matt) Chojecki

You'll always be my favourite brother.

CHAPTER 1

How do you disappear without a trace?

No clues left behind. No evidence. Nothing. One day you're going on about your business. The next, you've vanished into thin air. Poof and you're gone.

Maybe, Ava Reed thought, the better question was why. There were three fundamental reasons someone vanished. You either disappeared because you wanted to, something happened that made you forget who you were, or someone made damned sure you were gone forever.

She glanced at the framed picture on her desk. A young woman holding a small girl in her arms stared back at her. Sharon Novak. Brilliant student. Accused embezzler and criminal mastermind. Her mother.

Which one was it for you, Sharon?

Ava stared at the photo just like she has done so many times over the years. Sharon's dark hair, much like her own, fell over her shoulder, curling slightly at the ends. She had one of those thousand-watt smiles and a twinkle in her blue eyes. Little Ava sat on her lap, smiling shyly at the camera, her little hand curled around the pendant on her mother's necklace. Yet, the woman holding her was a stranger.

She touched the pendant, now hanging around her neck. The emerald-cut tourmaline stone was set in gold with four-split prongs on top and bottom. It was suspended from a gold chain with a delicately ornate loop. The gem always reminded her of aged whiskey. Sharon inherited it from her grandmother, and now Ava wore it around her neck. It was the most tangible link to her mother she still had.

Driven by her own need to find Sharon, Ava dedicated her life to working with missing person organizations and groups across Canada and the United States. She knew the grief, the pain and hope those left behind carried with them. Few ever got their answers, and for those that did, those answers weren't always the ones they hoped for. But at least they got closure. It was more than she ever did.

Several years ago, she set up a website in hopes of finding her mother. Every now and then, she received messages from random strangers claiming to have spotted Sharon. According to some of them, she was living in South America. Others claim to have seen her in Asia or somewhere in the Australian Outback. She was either living large on a yacht in the Mediterranean or had given up her worldly possessions for a simple life in a Tibetan monastery. So far, none of the sightings turned up anything useful.

Ava closed her eyes and let go of the pendant. She pinched the bridge of her nose with two fingers. The brewing headache meant that she had spent way too much time staring at her computer screen. It's been a long few days.

She stared absently out the window. The sun was setting over the Halifax harbour, her temporary home. A few months ago, she came to Nova Scotia to work on a few cases for her podcast, The Missing Voices. She ended up staying longer as more cases caught her attention. With thousands of people going missing each year in Canada, they all piled up, especially when the leads dried up. Most cops, despite their best efforts, moved on to new cases while the family members continued to search for answers. That's where she came in.

The podcast became Ava's obsession and her mission in life. It was a way for her to help others look for their loved ones. To give the missing a voice. It was an outlet for her own painful loss, and it gave her a focus. Selfishly, she hoped that one day it would help her get her own answers.

An incoming video call snapped her back to reality. She accepted the call from her new producer, Lori and smiled. Lori was assigned to her by Odyssey, the communication network that brought her podcast into their fold. So far, she was worth her weight in gold.

"Lori!" she said. "How goes it?"

Lori's dark and clever eyes narrowed as she took a closer look at the screen and adjusted her oversized glasses. "Have you been working yourself to death again? You look like crap, Ava."

"Well, hello to you too."

"Seriously, have you given some thought to finally hiring an assistant?" Lori's gaze was unshakeable. She then took her glasses off, which signalled she meant business. Ava often suspected Lori wore them to project that sexy librarian look, not because she really needed them. "You're not doing it all by yourself anymore. You have a budget. Use it."

"Yeah, yeah," Ava ran her hand through her messy mop of hair. Lori, who always seemed so put together, always made her feel like a hot mess. But while she could've passed as Naomi Campbell's little sister, Lori didn't have a mean bone in her body.

"I told you I'll think about it," Ava rolled her eyes. "I don't have time to train some newbie who gets squeamish about death."

"Get one that doesn't," Lori offered. "There are plenty of people out there who are not afraid of death and murder and don't mind working around it."

"Yeah, they're called serial killers."

Lori gave her a pained look. "I meant like cops, private investigators and such. I'm sure you can find someone who used to be one or maybe wants to become one."

"I really don't think either demographic would be my first choice."

"What exactly is your first choice then? Give me what you are looking for, and I will find you some candidates."

Ava thought about the offer. All she ever wanted to do was tell stories. Until Lori and the Odyssey team came along, she was doing everything herself. The research, the notes, reaching out to contacts and setting up interviews. Then she had to do the recording and editing.

Now she handed off the behind-the-scenes work to Lori and her team. They were highly organized and made Ava's job a lot easier. There was no way she could handle it all herself anymore. Lori was a fantastic resource and a huge asset, but she wasn't there to help Ava with day-to-day things. Maybe that assistant wasn't that bad of an idea after all.

"Okay, fine," she said. "I need someone who can think on their feet, can follow directions, but at the same time, I want them to have initiative. I don't want a pushover, and I don't want to be told what to do either."

"That's simple enough," Lori said as she scribbled down Ava's requirements. "Leave it with me. If you think of anything else, send it to me. Meanwhile, I'll get you some candidates to interview."

"Great, now can we talk about the new season?"

"Absolutely. I got all the files you sent over. I'll get the production team rolling. We'll put on some finishing touches and release it shortly. Based on what I've seen so far, I think we got another great one on our hands."

Ava smiled. She worked her butt off in the last few months and felt good about the work. The stories of the missing always drew her in. Figuring out the why's and how's was what she thrived on. Especially when those missing turned up dead.

They talked shop for a few more minutes about the upcoming schedule. Ava was tasked with spreading the word, research and the actual storytelling. Hyping up the podcast on other shows and online true crime communities was something she enjoyed more than the production. However, it was probably a good time to take some time off before jumping on the cases for the next season.

After the call, Ava briefly checked her email. She responded to urgent messages and skimmed the rest. They could wait till tomorrow. She looked at her face in the mirror. The dark bags under her eyes were the size of craters. Perhaps Lori was right. She needed some sleep. Resigned, Ava headed to bed and slept like the dead.

***

After working non-stop for months, it always felt strange to wake up and have nothing to do. Ava stretched a bit longer than usual and stared at the ceiling, debating whether she should just stay in bed all day. Tempting as it was, she really needed to get up.

She finally made it out of bed and went straight for the shower. Over breakfast, Ava checked her messages, answered emails and touched base with Lori one more time. As much as she wanted to dive into more work, it was probably better to go outside and get some fresh air. It was a gorgeous day, and it would be a shame to waste it.

Ava threw a green hoodie over a black tank top and matching tights. She tied her hair in a messy bun and put on her headphones. She selected the appropriate playlist, hit play and set the phone in her armband. She loved running. It was a great way to clear her head. Running also got her heartbeat up, making her feel alive.

It didn't take long to reach the boardwalk. The Halifax waterfront was always an exciting place to hang out and people watch. Slightly out of breath and drenched in sweat, Ava stopped to stretch out by one of the empty benches.

It was a busy day downtown, and the boardwalk was filled with people strolling along. Locals and tourists alike spilled in and out of the local bars, shops and restaurants. Couples, families, friends, strangers. Some rode their bikes while others sat around people watching. Every one of them living blissfully in the moment.

Ava grabbed a bottle of water from one of the food stalls and decided to cool down before heading back home to change. She joined the crowds walking along the boardwalk and soaked up the sunshine. The harbour was filled with boats of all sizes as they glided across the water. Ferries and cruise boats, packed with tourists snapping pictures from the water and getting splashed in the process, made rounds in the harbour. It was another summer day in the city.

Ava made her way past the playgrounds, stalls and attractions, planning on turning around at the large parking lot near the water. She paused when she noticed a small crowd of onlookers gathering nearby. Curious, Ava decided to investigate what's going on instead of heading back. She was, after all, as intrigued as the others.

"I bet you it's another car," she heard an older woman in a blue tracksuit and white running shoes say to her companion. She was short and plump with short grayish hair and way too much makeup. She wore a white visor and a fanny pack where she undoubtedly stored her lipstick and keys.

"You think so?" her friend replied with an unmistakable glee in her voice. She, too, had on a similar outfit as her friend, although less rosy cheeks. Hers was pink, and instead of a fanny pack, she had a small purse draped over her shoulder. Ava doubted either one of them actually did any working out. "I wonder if there is a dead body inside."

"Mary," her companion scolded, but it was clear that she, too, hoped that was the case. Ava could almost see her rubbing her manicured hands together in anticipation.

She moved closer to the two women as she tried to peer over the crowd. Being tall had its advantages. At five foot nine, she could easily see over the group gathered around the area police roped off with yellow tape. Several uniforms tried to keep the growing crowd at bay with various levels of success. From where she stood, Ava could see that there was definitely something in the water. Something large enough to require more than just a few uniforms to fish out.

"What do you mean, another car?" Ava asked. "Sorry," she added when the woman turned toward her. "I couldn't help overhearing your conversation."

They both seized her up with knowing glances.

"Well, it's not the first one. A few years back, they pulled another car out of the harbour." Mary said in a theatrical whisper and paused dramatically. "There was a dead body inside."

Mary's companion nodded enthusiastically. "It was a man. He'd been in the water for some time by the time they found him. I'm sure the fish would have got to him if he wasn't in the car," she added. "When was that they pulled him out again, Bonnie?"

"It was early 2008, I think," Bonnie said. "Or was it 2009?"

"Are you sure it wasn't 2007?" Mary wondered.

"No, I'm pretty sure it was 2009."

"How dreadful," Ava interrupted Bonnie and Mary's walk down the memory lane and made a mental note to check it out. "Did they ever find out who the man was?"

Both Mary and Bonnie seemed to consider her question, trying to recall the details.

"I'm pretty sure he wasn't from around here. Definitely out of province." Mary provided. "They ID'd him and all, but I can't remember the man's name."

"That's right!" Bonnie was clearly enjoying rehashing the story of a dead guy who happened to meet his end in the icy waters. "He was from Ontario or maybe Quebec? Definitely not from Nova Scotia. So many people come here from all over, it's hard to keep track."

The women continued to debate over the details of that day and which province the dead man came from. Ava excused herself and left them to it. She made her way closer to the water, trying to eavesdrop on what the cops said about the discovery, but didn't have much luck.

Torn between curiosity and dismay, Ava debated whether she should stick around or head home. It was just like her to stumble upon a mystery. The darkness always seemed to follow her everywhere, even without trying. It was unavoidable, like an obsession. At least that was what her boyfriend, Tom, told her many years ago before he dumped her for a cheerful kindergarten teacher.

According to Tom, death and murder were drawn to her like a moth to a flame. She was always fixated on the stories of the missing and the forgotten. She cared more about them than the people in her life. So much so, he said, that she was incapable of forming healthy attachments with others.

He wasn't all wrong. That's what happened when your mother walked out of your life when you were five. She didn't expect him to understand that. Then again, few ever did, and that's why she tended to avoid long-term relationships.

She spent enough years in therapy to understand that Sharon's disappearance had nothing to do with anything she did or said. While the memories still stung a little, Ava decided that maybe she didn't need to try to solve every problem she came across. Like the possible car in the harbour. The cops could handle it. Body or no body, this had nothing to do with her.

Ava decided to head back. The sudden rumbling in her stomach reminded her that it was time to eat. She weighed her options and opted for takeout. Later that evening, Ava watched the news as she packed. There was a short segment on the discovery in the lake. It turned out to be a car that the police thought was part of an illegal shipment heading overseas, which apparently wasn't that uncommon. Whether it was dumped accidentally or on purpose wasn't really her concern.

The news anchor quickly referenced the car found in 2009 with human remains, which aligned with what Mary and Bonnie told her. Adult male in mid-forties from Ontario.

Not a pleasant way to die, she thought as she made transportation arrangements for the following day. It was time to leave Halifax.

***

It was construction season in Toronto. It went hand in hand with the hot and sticky days of summer in the city. That meant the humidity was already high, and it was barely morning. In his trailer, Sam Ellis wiped the sweat off his forehead with the back of his hand as he set his safety helmet on the desk. As the construction site supervisor, he was responsible for all aspects of the Silver Clover project, from scheduling work and maintaining records to ensuring all work stayed on budget.

He's been working in construction for what seemed like a lifetime. While his job required more and more computer work, he still loved every aspect of it. The Silver Clover was a high-profile development project with lots of money thrown at it and lots of political interest.

Sam smiled. He hated politics, but he liked his job, and as long as the NorFast Group was willing to employ him, he'll keep working. He grabbed his cup and took a sip. The coffee was lukewarm, which suited him just fine.

As far as construction projects went, this one was pretty much like every other project Sam has worked on. The southeast corner of Front and Cherry Streets would become another condo development, taking over the last vacant spots in the neighbourhood. Known as the West Don Lands, this was once home to heavy industry and warehouses. It eventually turned into a derelict area after the industry shut down. What a difference a few decades make.

Looking at the shiny new condos, parks and shops, it was hard to imagine this area before the gentrification. Once a place filled with dirt, despair and the desperate who lived on the fringes of humanity, it was now an active part of Toronto's downtown where tourists and locals came in droves.

Today, the nearby Distillery District only added to the artsy vibe of the area. What was once the biggest distillery in the British Empire had been transformed into a pedestrian-only neighbourhood with condos, shops, restaurants and one of the biggest Christmas markets in the city.

Sam spent the morning dealing with progress reports, contractor schedules, and shipment verifications. He looked up at the sudden commotion outside. The door swung open, and Johnny Alves, one of the younger workers on the site, stood there nervously. His eyes were wide as saucers.

"Holy shit, Sam," he blurted out. "You gotta come and see this."

Unfazed, Sam looked up and stretched the kink in his neck. His crew wasn't prone to drama, but the heat had a way of making some pretty jumpy. You never knew what kind of nonsense a bunch of grown-ass men could come up with. It wouldn't be the first time he had to break apart a couple of hotheads on his site.

"What is it, Johnny?"

"It looks like we got a..." he said almost in a whisper that took Sam a few seconds to register. "We got a dead body."

"You're shitting me," he didn't have to be told twice. Sam was up and out of the trailer with Johnny at his heels.

As the site was relatively small, it didn't take them long to reach a group of men gathered around. They loitered around, looking and pointing at something in the ground with various degrees of curiosity and dismay.

Sam pushed his way through and looked down what looked like an old shaft or a well. Few meters down, under rubble and dirt, lay a human skull sticking out of the ground. It was hard to tell how long it's been there, but whoever it was, they likely have been there for some time.

"Sweet Jesus," he closed his eyes, trying not to puke. The last thing he needed was to contaminate the scene. He's seen enough crime shows to know about the issues that could cause. Plus, it would be embarrassing to cast his stomach contents in front of the guys.

Instead, he focused on moving everyone away from the immediate area and leaving the scene to the professionals. Groaning inside at the thought of the piles of paperwork and reports this discovery would undoubtedly add to his day, he took out his phone and dialled 911.

It didn't take long for the cops to show up. It was clear that the site would be shut down not just for the day but for quite some time. Determining who the remains belonged to would take longer. This area was once full of drug addicts, dealers and other shady characters. Any one of them could have ended down there.

It didn't take long for white tents to go up. They covered the area where the remains were found, blocking the scene from news choppers flying overhead. Cops were crawling everywhere while techs in white suits did their thing. The only remaining building on the site that would be incorporated into the new building now acted as a makeshift office where police collected statements from the crew.

In the distance, a crowd gathered by the fence erected around the construction site. News crews were already setting up their equipment while curious onlookers in the surrounding condos peered nonchalantly through their windows. Others were more obvious, filming as much as possible on their balconies. This was going to be a shitshow for the suits at NorFast, nothing the hotshots in the PR department couldn't deal with.

Sam unscrewed the cap on his water bottle and downed most of the content. As there wasn't much else to do at the moment, he headed back to his trailer to start on that incident report.

***

Across town, Elizabeth Northam sat at her sleek desk in the elegant offices of the NorFast Group. Her office overlooked the city's downtown core with the shimmering waters of Lake Ontario in the distance. Usually, the views relaxed her, but today, she barely registered what she was looking at.

Elizabeth, in her meticulous navy power suit and matching skinny heels, was not prone to hysterics. Her life, much like her flawless makeup and perfectly coiffed hair, permanently dyed a perfect shade of honey blonde, was perfectly organized and planned out. She's been running this company for over a decade, and she wasn't ready to give up the power.

She dug her cell phone out of the massive purse that sat on her desk and punched in a number. It rang several times before the call was answered on the other end.

"We have a problem at the site," she said simply without any trace of emotion. "How soon can you be here?"

The call was short and to the point. Satisfied with the response, Elizabeth slid the phone back into her purse and slowly got up. She walked outside to the area dedicated to the Silver Clover project. It was just as sleek as the rest of the office, with lots of white space and tasteful décor.

Elizabeth personally overlooked the room setup where a miniature model of the development was displayed on a massive table in the centre. On the walls were the artist's renderings, samples and blueprints that she used every day to ensure her company's vision came to life.

She walked around the table, admiring her vision. This was going to be one of her best developments yet. A sure way to move her company into a very bright future.

A girl can't run a construction company. Her father's voice echoed in her mind as if he was here in the room with her. She pushed the voice away. If he could only see her now.

The discovery of the remains put a slight hitch in the project, but Elizabeth was sure she could get it moving forward as planned. Her dark eyes narrowed like a ready to pounce on its prey. There was no way she would let it all fall apart now.

CHAPTER 2

Ava left Halifax and flew straight to London, her home away from home. Her father and stepmother have lived here for as long as she could remember. Growing up, it was often tricky having to split time between staying in London with her parents and in Toronto with her grandparents. Still, all the adults somehow made it work, and so did she.

Ava didn't have a place of her own, and that never bothered her. She was never in one place long enough for it to stick. That one failed attempt to live with Tom, and several short-lived relationships that followed made her realize that it was a lot easier not to rely on others. With no boyfriends demanding her time and a handful of friends, Ava was left to her own devices and to what she did best, solving missing cases.

Her parents lived in a posh townhouse in Kensington, which was close to Hyde Park. Ava loved running here. Sometimes she incorporated routes in Hyde Park with Kensington Gardens, completing the entire loop around the parameter. Today, Ava didn't bother with any of the attractions along the way and kept it simple. She needed to run.

Ava enjoyed coming to London. It was large enough to keep her busy and offered enough distractions to fill the time. Occasionally, she went out with some acquaintances or even squeezed in a date. But on this visit, she was getting restless. Sometimes, vacations were overrated.

Satisfied with her run, Ava made her way home. Her parents lived in a stunning three-level townhouse with a pretty red brick exterior. In spring, the neighbourhood was filled with blooming wisterias that added a romantic vibe to the street. Nice digs if you can get them.

Her stepmother, Joan, came from money, and the property has been in her family for an impressively long time. As a well-known interior designer, Joan knew everyone worth knowing in London. She was the doting corporate wife when it was required and the tony socialite when it suited her. She loved to garden and frequently hosted lavish parties. Over the years, they developed a friendly relationship that served them both. Joan fussed over Ava and dragged her to spas whenever she could. She never tried to take over as Ava's mother, choosing to play the friend role instead.

The first time she met Joan, Ava was about six or seven. She was fascinated by her father's new friend, who spoke funny and looked like something out of a magazine. Over the years,

Ava got accustomed to Joan's posh accent, but the memory of that initial meeting still made her smile.

She found them having tea in the parlour off the kitchen. Even though it was a Saturday morning, both were dressed impeccably as they enjoyed their tea. Her father was dressed in casual slacks and a white Polo shirt, while Joan wore a fitting yellow dress that cut off just below the knees. Her blonde shoulder-length bob bounced slightly as she set her cup on the saucer in front of her.

Her father spotted her first as he looked up from his paper. His dark eyes met hers across the room as he folded the paper and set it on the table.

"Did you have a good run?" he asked.

"Yeah, it was great," Ava grinned at him. "You should have come."

She grabbed a plate from one of the cabinets in the kitchen and joined them at the table. Joan reached for the teapot as Ava filled her plate with food.

"Tea?" she asked, and Ava nodded in agreement.

Michael Reed watched his daughter absently as she doctored her tea. It still jolted him sometimes at how closely she resembled her mother. She was taller, probably getting the height from him, but her mannerisms were all Sharon. Both could be persistently insistent, like a dog with a bone. Fiercely independent and stubborn as hell.

While Sharon was friendly and outgoing, Ava was more reserved and introverted. She often came across as aloof and had a hard time making friends. It was even more challenging for her after Sharon went missing. Michael spent years worrying about his daughter and always tried to fill the void left by her mother.

She got the love of running from him. Sharon never cared for it, so after she left, he introduced his daughter to his hobby. These days he preferred to run on his treadmill while Ava opted for the outdoors. It's been a while since they went running together.

"Maybe I can join you for a run tomorrow," he said. "That way, I can see how out of shape you really are."

"You're on," Ava grinned. "Just don't start crying when I leave you in the dust."

"Oh, I highly doubt that," he laughed.

As they planned, Joan poured herself another cup of tea. She listened with amusement as they argued over the best route and the distance. She wasn't a runner herself, but she could appreciate the joy it brought them.

"We're thinking of heading to the Hawthorn House for the day," she said when they stopped arguing. "It's that gorgeous estate just outside town. I think we went there before on one of your previous visits. Since it's a nice day, we thought of making a day out of it. Would you care to join us?"

Ava was tempted to decline, hoping to do some more digging into the new cases that Lori sent over. She also needed to look over the candidates Lori emailed. But they both seemed so hopeful. Work could wait for another day or so, she decided. Sometimes family obligations came first.

"Sure," she said as she wiped her mouth with a napkin. "Let me shower and get ready."

When she left, Joan patted her husband's hand with her own. They exchanged knowing looks. "She looks more and more like Sharon," he said absently.

"I know. But she's not Sharon, Michael," she replied. "You have to remember that."

***

Hawthorn House was as stunning as the National Trust brochure described. Joan was a huge supporter of the initiative because it focused on preserving the numerous historic sites, properties and green spaces. All things near and dear to her heart. As a member, she used her privileges frequently and always insisted that Ava visited at least one property when she was in town.

While she didn't share her stepmother's passion for architecture and design, Ava always enjoyed the outings. Being there made Joan happy, and that was a small price to pay for a few hours of running around some random old estate. After all, it wasn't a hardship to stroll around perfectly manicured gardens and see how the rich used to live. Plus, it was always fun to see Joan ooh and ahh over some old tapestry, furniture or knickknack.

Joan was still chatting excitedly about the stunning interiors and delightful gardens when they got home. Her father nodded patiently and made appropriate sounds of delight and agreement. Ava wondered how long it would take Joan to redecorate again. It wouldn't be the first time she got inspired by a grand manor house or a museum.

She headed downstairs to the lower level where her room was located. The sun was still peeking through the windows, bathing the area in a warm glow. Ava contemplated sitting outside as she checked her emails but decided against it. They would likely sit outside after dinner anyway.

Ava plugged her phone in to charge, then changed from her sundress into jeans and a t-shirt. Unlike Joan, she preferred to be out of a dress. The house was nice and cool inside, and the tiled floors felt refreshing under her bare feet. She ditched the heels the moment they got back.

Somewhere inside the house, the phone rang. She absently heard her father pick up as she scrolled through her emails. As Ava debated whether she could squeeze in a few hours of work after dinner, she heard Joan calling for her. She poked her head out the door as Joan's voice became more urgent. She felt a sudden chill creep down her spine. It was not like Joan to raise her voice like that.

Ava went upstairs and stopped as she got into the living room. Her father, his face white as a ghost, still held the phone in his hand. When he saw her, she saw tears in his eyes. Something was wrong.

"Grandpa?" she asked.

"No," he said, his voice barely a whisper. "It's Sharon. They found Sharon."

Part of her already knew the answer. The small glimmer of hope that hung by a thread faded away.

"Where?"

Ava didn't hear Joan walk up beside her until she placed her arm gently around Ava's shoulder. There was no easy way to do this.

"I'm sorry, darling," she whispered. "She's dead. Sharon isn't coming back."

"No." Ava looked at her father, waiting for confirmation. He nodded slowly.

"They found human remains on a construction site in Toronto not too long ago. They have just confirmed that it is Sharon." He said as he faced his daughter. "She's been dead all this time. They think someone killed her, Ava. I'm so sorry."

Blinded by the sudden tears, Ava grabbed onto the armchair to steady herself. They made a mistake. Sharon couldn't be dead. She lived with anger, pain, and even hate all these years towards a woman she thought had abandoned her.

Instead, she was chasing a ghost. Sharon had been dead all this time. She never left. The realization cut deep.

Michael put his arms around his daughter as she cried. He did the same when she was five. Back then, she called for her mother, not understanding why she was gone. Ava screamed and cried for months, demanding to see Sharon. It almost killed him to see his daughter so distraught back then. Today, the pain was just as raw.

It's been almost twenty-five years. His heart broke for his little girl all over again. Sharon wasn't perfect and had her flaws, but Michael didn't know if he ever believed that she abandoned her child. Maybe it was easier to think that she did rather than to think the worse. But the worst did happen, and now they had to deal with it.

Time seemed to slow down. It could have been minutes or hours since her world shattered. When she felt like no more tears were left, Ava let her father guide her back to the chair. She sunk into the thick cushions, feeling like she was in a daze. Joan forced a glass of whiskey into her hand and told her to drink it.

Ava sat silently, flanked by her father on one side and Joan on the other. She downed the whiskey and tried not to puke as the liquid burned her throat. Thankfully Joan also made tea which she poured for all of them.

"What happened?" Ava asked her father. "Does Grandpa know?"

"Yes," Michael smiled through his own tears, thinking of his father-in-law. "Stan's the one that called and," he held up his hand when she tried to get up, "I told him you'll call him back."

"Are they sure it's her?"

"Yes, the DNA test has confirmed it. I'm sorry, Ava."

"Do they know what happened?" She knew they likely didn't, at least not right away.

"No, I don't think so. I assume that there will be an investigation."

"I have to go back to Toronto," Ava said. "I want to call Grandpa, and then I need to book my flight."

Michael and Joan watched her leave the room. Joan reached over to her husband and squeezed his hand.

"She's going to be okay, Michael. She's strong, and she has us and Stan to help her get through this."

He looked at his wife, her soft green eyes watching him carefully. "I really hoped this would end differently."

***

Across the pond, Nick Laskaris wished he was anywhere but in Toronto. It was another hot day in the city, with everyone trying to escape the muggy heat of the summer. It was patio season, and everyone was desperate for a table.

The patio at The Acropolis, the Laskaris family restaurant, was also packed. The evening crowds came out to gossip and celebrate over a cold drink. He fondly remembered serving tables here as a teenager when his parents still actively run the restaurant. These days, the restaurant was mainly in his uncle Kostas and aunt Maria's hands while his parents spent the summers in Greece with his brother George and his family.

Nick still loved coming to the restaurant. It was a place where his family and friends gathered regularly. However, on busy days like today, he was glad his passion took him elsewhere.

As a kid, he fell in love with an old camera one of his cousins passed down to him. Nick had discovered that he had a knack for the creative. He loved seeing the world through a lens and marvelled at the many ways it can be manipulated. He took pictures, and later video, of everything around him, annoying the shit out of everyone in his family.

He's come a long way since those days. He had several cameras, tripods, a case filled with lenses and enough accessories to fill a shop. He tried getting a "real" job that his parents would approve of, but after years of working a desk job for others, Nick finally decided to do his own thing. Luckily for him, he had no shortage of clients demanding his services. He was his own boss and loved every minute of it.

Nick still frequented the restaurant and helped out when he could. That often meant running the food or clearing tables. Especially on evenings like today, when it was busier than usual. Just like everyone else, he didn't feel like making dinner, so he came here instead. If clearing a few tables meant that he would be fed, it was a win-win solution for everyone.

Toronto's vibrant Greektown neighbourhood was always a popular destination for tourists and hungry locals. The Acropolis sat on the north side of Danforth Avenue as it has for over a decade. While many restaurants and storefronts expanded to include different flavours and ethnicities, most were still full of Greek influences.

As the restaurant got busier, Nick fell into a familiar routine. He made small talk with the regulars, flirted with the occasional friendly customer and chatted it up with friends who dropped by. What he really wanted was a smoke. Nick gave up smoking years ago, but every now and then, the itch would come back. Today was one of those days.

He looked over at the patio as he rubbed his hand on his scruffy jaw. Since things looked under control, he decided it was time for a break. Inside, his cousin Steve minded the bar. Nick headed right over and grabbed a seat. The cool breeze from the air conditioning fell over him like a lovely, airy waterfall. Steve grabbed a cold beer out of the fridge and set it in front of him.

"Why aren't you in Greece?" He asked as he wiped the bar with a towel. "It feels like hell here right now."

Nick took a long sip of the ice-cold beer. Steve wasn't wrong, it did feel like hell, and he was smackdown in the middle of it. Maybe he should have gone to Greece with his parents after all. He could have been hanging out at the beach instead of melting in Toronto.

"I could ask you the same thing," Nick said. "Turns out we're both suckers for staying here instead of living it up on some island in Greece."

"Unlike you, I can't take my work with me," Steve reminded him. "What's your excuse? Are you tired of your mother trying to set you up again?"

Nick rolled his eyes and rubbed his temples. "I have had enough of my mother's schemes to hook me up with girls she thinks are good for me. I can manage on my own."

"Ah, but how else are you supposed to find a wife, pretty boy?" Steve grinned at his cousin, silently grateful that he had a girlfriend to keep his parents off his back. The ladies seemed to like his cousin's scruffy good looks and charming smile, even if he was mostly oblivious to it.

"I don't need a wife," Nick said with a shrug. "After what happened with Nicole, I think I'm going to stay clear of relationships. Plenty of women out there. I can totally go for some casual dating. You know, easy and uncomplicated. Someone who is nice, chilled and doesn't want to run my life."

"Nicole wasn't really a good match for you, bro," Steve said as he wiped the bar. "But easy and uncomplicated? I don't think that's your style, no matter what you say."

"You think I like complicated relationships? What am I? A glutton for punishment?"

"Easy gets boring very fast. You like a challenge. Nicole wasn't a challenge. She attached herself to you as soon as you looked her way. Besides," he pointed out, "hooking up and relationships are different. Choose wisely."

"When did you become such a relationship guru?" Nick asked. "You get a girlfriend, and all of a sudden, you're giving everyone love advice?"

"Ah, I said nothing about love," Steve winked at him. "That is all you."

"Love has nothing to do with this." Nick rolled his eyes and downed the rest of his beer while Steve got busy getting drink orders for the waiters.

He didn't need a matchmaker, and he definitely wasn't looking for a relationship. The truth was, he was bored. He needed some excitement, or he would die from boredom.

He was about to call it a night and head out when a "breaking news" banner flashed on the news. He grabbed the remote and turned up the volume on the TV.

"The remains found on the construction site in the city earlier this summer have been positively identified as those of Sharon Novak. The twenty-nine-year-old woman went missing in late October 1995. Novak mysteriously disappeared, and so did three million dollars from her employer's account. Police can now confirm that the death wasn't accidental, and the deceased's family has been notified. Stay tuned as we follow the investigation."

A photo of Sharon flashed on the screen. The news anchor encouraged anyone with information about her disappearance to contact the police. Nick turned the volume down as the news moved on to another subject.

"Wasn't it that the woman who lived next door to you guys?" Steve asked as he came up beside Nick.

"Yeah, she was Mr. Novak's daughter. She lived there for a while with her kid." He remembered talking to her a few times before she went missing. In his twelve-year-old mind, she was the hottest woman he knew. She was also kind and smiled a lot. "I can't believe she's dead."

Nick thought of his neighbour, Mr. Novak and how this news must have shocked him. Many theories were going around when Sharon went missing. Most of them didn't paint her in a positive light. Over the years, the Novaks staunchly defended their daughter, refusing to believe she ran away with stolen money. Looks like they might have been right. He made a note to check on his neighbour.

"I gotta go," he said.

Nick's mind was suddenly filled with unexpected memories of a dead woman and the old man still living next door to his childhood home. Maybe it wasn't his place to get involved, but he couldn't just sit there and do nothing.

***

The news report stirred a lot of old memories. Across town, someone else was watching the news about Sharon with little enthusiasm. A glass flew across the room and shattered as it hit the wall spilling the amber liquid all over the floor.

After almost twenty-five years, one would think the story would have gone away, but no. Here she was again, making waves. Sharon Novak.

Sharon was a nosy busybody who had a habit of sticking her nose where it didn't belong. Always asking questions, hanging out with the wrong people and pushing too many buttons.

Sharon had many valuable skills, but she wasn't indispensable. She always thought that she was smarter than everyone else and could do whatever she wanted without consequences. If she had only learned to stay out of things, life would have turned out differently.

Hopefully, her daughter was smart enough not to repeat her mother's mistakes. Otherwise, she'd end up like Sharon.

Sometimes, no matter how much you tried, the past just wouldn't stay buried.

CHAPTER 3

They flew to Toronto the next day. Between meeting with the police, organizing a memorial service for Sharon and dealing with the fact that she wasn't coming back, reality started to set in.

It was almost a relief when they finally said goodbye to Sharon. Ava wasn't sure she could take any more grief. They all remembered her in their ways, except for Ava. She had no memories to comfort her. A box with her mother's remains was the closest she would ever get to the woman who gave her life.

The small ceremony brought a sense of peace but no closure as they had hoped for. Michael and Joan flew back to London right after while Ava stayed with her grandfather in Toronto. They met with Detective Burnett, the man in charge of Sharon's investigation, hoping for answers. As it turned out, he had more questions than answers.

Stan Novak watched his granddaughter pace in the living room. She was tall and lanky, her dark hair pulled back in a messy braid. Long bangs hung like curtains, swinging gently with every step.

He wrung his hands in frustration just as Ava jammed hers in the pockets of her jeans.

"Oh, do sit down, Ava," he said. "I'm getting tired watching you."

She stopped and whirled around. Stan hooked his reading glasses on the V-neck of his button-up shirt. He was a slender and short man, but he was still full of energy and sharp as ever. He had a mop of silver hair and piercing blue eyes. No matter what life threw at him, Stan always tried to figure things out like they were a puzzle. His seemingly endless patience often annoyed Ava, especially when it came to finding Sharon.

As a professor of classical studies, Stan was used to dealing with the lives of people who have been dead for centuries. His work was all about rediscovering, learning and understanding the philosophies, history and art of the ancient Greeks and Romans. Studying the surviving artifacts, searching for clues and interpreting the data taught him to be a patient man. Well, that and age. Now that he was retired and in his seventies, he looked at life differently. He didn't have decades left to learn what happened to his daughter, and he wasn't going to waste that time he had.

"I just don't understand, Grandpa," Ava said in frustration, stopping for a moment. "How can they claim not to know anything? She's been missing for almost twenty-five years. What have they been doing all this time?"

Stan could understand his granddaughter's frustration as she stood there, annoyed. He shared that feeling and wasn't satisfied with how Sharon's case was handled by the investigators. But he also knew that things could get cloudy very fast, hampering the search for the truth. Sometimes it was hard to find a middle ground between frustration and patience.

"You know as well as I do that these things take time," he told her. He, too, pestered the detectives on the case for answers, getting nowhere. "Back in 1995, this was a missing person's case, not a murder investigation. It doesn't excuse the way the investigation was handled, but we can't change the past."

Ava stood still, considering his words. He could feel the energy bursting from her. It made him dizzy. There was anger there, but he could also see the wheels turning in her head. The missing pieces of a larger puzzle stared at them like giant gaping holes. Just like him, Ava liked puzzles. She needed to solve this puzzle even more than he did.

"So, basically, they wasted all this time," she said with disgust. "They never bothered getting any evidence because it was easier to believe that she ran away. Meanwhile, she's been here all this time."

She started pacing again. Stan didn't have insights into what the cops knew and how they went about their investigation. God knows he tried to find, but the freedom of information act requests he submitted over the years got him nowhere.

Stan still remembered the pain of losing his parents and cherished the memories he had of them. His wife's death devastated him, but he was grateful for the years they spent together. He carried the memories of his daughter in his heart and mind, hoping that one day he would see her again. Now that he knew Sharon wasn't coming back, it felt like his heart was breaking all over again. But he was thankful that there was so much of Sharon in her daughter. In a small way, it lessened his pain.

As he watched Ava, he wondered what a toll this loss took on her. Living in the shadow of a woman she never got a chance to know. They all became blinded by their own pain that they overlooked hers. Ava was such a quiet child, very unlike Sharon at that age. She was a distraught and hurt little girl that grew up to be an inquisitive and compassionate woman standing before him.

"Ava," he got up, frustrated by her pacing and motioned for her to come and sit. "The police will be meeting with us soon. They share with us what they know, and hopefully, we'll know more."

"That's if they even bother to tell us the truth."

"You know, your mother would be very proud of you."

"You think?"

"Absolutely. Listen, I know that as her father, I'm a bit biased," Stan told her. "But she was a good person, no matter what they say. Sharon always believed in doing the right thing. It's how we raised her. Don't forget it."

Ava nodded. She really wanted to believe that her mother wasn't a thief and a liar. There were so many sides to Sharon, and they changed depending on who you talked to. She hoped to find the one closest to the real woman one day, but she was doubtful it would ever happen.

"Ava, this is what you do. You help search for missing people," her grandfather reminded her. "Investigate this like you do all your cases. We'll leave the police to do their job, but that doesn't mean we stop investigating ourselves. We have a huge advantage here."

She smiled at him in that Sharon-like way. "You're right. We know what happened to her. We now have to figure out the who and the why."

For the first time in a very long time, Stan Novak felt like there was a light to guide him out of this darkness. He wasn't a religious man, but right now, he thanked whoever was out there for the gift that was his granddaughter.

"You know," he added with a smile. "Your grandmother never stopped believing that Sharon would one day come back. She even kept many of her things in boxes."

They exchanged knowing looks and sly smiles. It was going to be okay, Stan thought. Together they would find the answers. They would do right by Sharon.

"So, what are we waiting for?" She flashed him another smile, and they went to work.

***

After a couple of hours of searching, they didn't find anything useful. She left Stan to rest while she focused on interviewing another batch of potential assistants. So far, there wasn't even one single person that she wanted to hire. Granted, her criteria were broad, but Ava assumed Lori would be better at fielding the applications before passing them on to her.

Ava listened to the woman currently on her screen as she listed her accomplishments and virtues. She already interviewed about twenty people. None of them had what she was looking for. Ava wondered if Lori picked these people on purpose as if she wanted her to take on a more active role in finding someone. She would have to have a little talk with her producer.

"That's great, Hannah," Ava said without much enthusiasm. "You definitely have an impressive resume."

Hannah beamed at her and tucked her long, dark hair behind her ears. She leaned forward, ready for anything else Ava threw at her.

"I really need someone good at research. Like, really good," Ava said. "I need someone who can find information that isn't always easily available. Someone who can figure out how to get it. Do you know what I mean?"

"Oh, absolutely," Hannah clasped her hands together. "When I was in school, we did a lot of research and managed to find many things others didn't."

"That's great," Ava could feel a headache brewing. "Let's say I threw some cases at you and asked you to dig deep into them and get me info. How would you go about finding that information?"

"That's, like, totally easy," Hannah said. "I'd take the cases and sort them by what information is needed, in what order and by priority. Then I would assign them to appropriate interns. Once it was all collected, I'd put it together for you."

Ava just stared at her.

"I think you misunderstood," she said slowly. "There is nobody else. No interns. You are the person doing the research. I am looking for an assistant, not someone to delegate to other assistants."

Hannah's lips formed a surprised "oh," but she didn't have anything else to offer. That was the end of that interview. Next candidate listed true crime as his interests combined with a degree in computer science. He definitely had potential.

"So, Justin," Ava said. "Tell me why you're interested in this job?"

"Oh, man. I love true crime," he said enthusiastically. "I've, like, listened to every crime podcast out there. I love The Missing Voices. Plus, I've seen all the murder shows and stuff. I think I'd be really good at finding out who did it."

"I appreciate the enthusiasm," she told him. "How are your research skills?"

"Good, I think?" Justin said as if he was asking the question. "Will I be, like, you know, going with you to crime scenes? Seeing autopsies and busting up the bad guys? Oh," he perked up. "Do you work with hackers that break into secret government files?"

"No, to all of it."

Ava was tired. How difficult was it to find someone who can look for things, doesn't ask millions of questions and has realistic expectations? So far, most of the applicants she talked to had overactive imaginations and were more interested in playing armchair detectives rather than doing the grunt work.

Maybe she needed someone older, more mature. But age didn't always guarantee a more qualified candidate, as she found out.

"Tell me, Larry, why do you want this job?" she asked.

Larry stared at her with a look that bordered on disgust. He was balding, had thick glasses and an impressive moustache that matched the silver tufts of hair left on his head.

"I'm writing a thriller," he said as if he was talking to a child. "My agent suggested this gig as a great way to gather research for my book."

"You want this job so you can gather research for your book?" Ava echoed.

"Didn't I already say that?" he asked. "I need to know how detailed your notes are on the cases you work on. Will this job give me access to complete police files, autopsy reports and DNA samples?"

"Ugh…"

"I'll require access to everything you got. Police contacts would also be good to have, especially if they can provide access to the information I need," he continued as he listed his demands. "Medical professionals and the like would also work. I am especially interested in forensics and autopsies. So if you have those, I'd like to start with that. And," he leaned towards his screen and squinted at it. "To be clear, I don't work on weekends and need Mondays and Fridays off."

"I'll have to get back to you," Ava said and ended the call.

This was exhausting. Getting an assistant turned out to be a terrible idea. If having one meant she had to suffer all these people, she might be better off not hiring anyone.

***

Detective Tyler Burnett set down his green kale smoothie on his desk as he looked at his visitor. His short, brown hair was still damp from the shower he took at the gym at the station. He liked to stay fit by doing quick workouts at the station whenever he could before his shift. It helped him think.

"Thank you for coming in, Ms Reed," he said.

"Call me, Ava," she said. "What can you tell me about Sharon's investigation, Detective?"

"Right now, there isn't much that I can tell you," he said. "The information on your mother's case is minimal. It doesn't give me a lot to go on."

"Giving up already?" she asked with a smirk.

"I didn't say that," Tyler smiled. "Most of the cases that fall on my desk do so because the investigators were unable to solve them the first time around. Cases with lots of evidence, witnesses and viable suspects are rare and typically not the ones that go cold."

"So what now?" Ava asked. "Where do you start?"

Tyler smiled as he took a sip of his smoothie. Growing up, he always knew he wanted to be a cop, but not just any cop. He wanted to work on the old cases that sat on the shelves, waiting to be solved.

Tyler's grandfather, Benjamin Burnett, was a homicide detective with a long and successful career. He often talked about the cases he couldn't solve. They ate at him and followed him, still unresolved, into retirement. Tyler fondly remembered trying to help his grandfather solve the many puzzles. That was also the reason he made the decision to work the cold ones.

"At the beginning," he said and opened Sharon's file. "Sharon was reported missing by her parents on October 24, 1995. The Novaks, your grandparents, last saw their daughter four days earlier before they left with you for the cottage."

"Sounds about right," Ava agreed. She absently reached for the pendant on her necklace as if to connect to the past. "My parents recently divorced, and I moved in with my mother to my grandparents' home. I just turned five."

"It says here that your mother worked at a gallery, Studio 416," Tyler continued to read the file. "Her boss was a man named Adam Walker. Does that name ring a bell for you?"

"I've never met him," Ava said. "I just know the name from the reports."

"By all accounts," he continued, "Sharon was well-liked by everyone. Friends and coworkers spoke highly of her, but nobody could provide any clues as to what could have happened to her."

"I guess not everyone liked her," Ava said. "Otherwise, she wouldn't have ended up dead. Can you tell me how she died?"

There was no nice way to say it, so he just told her the truth. "She was shot. Judging by the bullet hole in her skull, someone wanted to make sure she stayed dead."

"Can I see the report?" she asked. When he didn't respond, Ava decided to try a different approach. "Look, maybe I can help. Finding missing people is what I do. I've worked with other police departments. There is no reason we can't do the same. I can give you references if you don't want to take my word for it."

Tyler considered her offer. He did some checking into Ava Reed already. She was an advocate for families with missing loved ones and became a true-crime podcaster. Not a massive stretch in his mind. He listened to a few episodes of The Missing Voices out of curiosity and found her approach thorough and unbiased.

"Look, I can get these reports one way or another," she said when he didn't answer. "But it would save a lot of time if you just gave them to me. I'm family. This is about my mother. I can help."

"I haven't said no, Ms Reed. Ava," he corrected when she opened her mouth to speak. "I don't have a problem working with you. In fact, I think that's a great idea."

"You do?"

"That surprises you?"

"Well, not everyone does."

"I like solving cases," he said. "And when it comes to the ones that have been lying on the shelf for decades, I'll take any help I can get."

"Then we have a deal," Ava smiled, pleased at the outcome. "I would like to speak to the original detective on Sharon's case," she said. "I haven't been able to locate him. Is that something you can get for me?"

"I should be able to get that," Tyler agreed. "Talking directly to Sharon's daughter might jog his memory. I'll also get you any reports that I can. Anything else?"

"I'd like to see where she was found."

"I can arrange that."

***

Nick got home late Saturday afternoon. He spent most of the morning on a photo shoot with a client. It was another hot day, and he was exhausted. His parents let him stay with them while he sorted out his living situation. Still, he really missed having his own space where he could keep all of his equipment permanently organized.

Nick figured he had enough time to shower and grab some food at The Acropolis before diving into today's footage. At this rate, he could leave the full edit for tomorrow after a quick call with the client first thing in the morning.

He unloaded the equipment in his makeshift office then jumped in the shower. There was nothing better than a cold one on a hot day like today. He let the water run over him, and when he started to feel human again, he turned off the tap and grabbed a towel. Ten minutes later, he was dressed in shorts and a t-shirt and on his way to the restaurant.

His parents' home sat on one of the streets that ran perpendicular to the Danforth and was a short walk from the restaurant. The street had big old trees on both sides of the road and was surprisingly quiet considering how busy the neighbourhood often got. Here children played outside, and dogs barked in excitement. Nick waved to neighbours in acknowledgement as they watered their gardens. Not much has changed since he was a kid.

The Acropolis was packed when he arrived, but everything seemed under control. Nick grabbed the bags with food and left before anyone stopped him to chat. He wasn't picky about the offerings, but today the bags seemed unusually heavy. His aunt gave him several dishes from a mixed-up takeout order the customer no longer wanted. This meant he had food for days. There was no way he was going to eat it all himself.

As he's done many times before, Nick walked over next door and rang the doorbell, trying to balance the bags as he did so. After Sharon was found, Nick kept his neighbour company more often, and the two developed a friendship of sorts.

But it wasn't Mr. Novak that answered the door.

She was taller than most women, but it wasn't the height that gave him pause. Her hair was jet black and carelessly pulled back with thick, long bangs that played peek-a-boo with a pair of sharp blue eyes. She had a striking face, high cheekbones and a piercing gaze that seemed to look right through him. She didn't seem overly friendly.

"We didn't order takeout," she said curtly, as one eyebrow shot up and disappeared somewhere underneath those bangs. "You got the wrong house."

"Whoa, wait a minute," he said before she slammed the door in his face. "I'm Nick. Nick from next door?" He added as if that clarified things.

She blinked, but before she had a chance to respond, Mr. Novak appeared at the door. Relieved, Nick shifted his gaze to him.

"Hey, Mr. Novak, I got loads of takeout from the restaurant and thought you might want to have some," he flashed a smile as he lifted the bags to show him. "Still hot."

"Yes, yes. Come, come in," Stan waved him in. "Nick, you remember my granddaughter Ava?"

"Sure do. How is it going?"

Ava didn't look impressed, nor did she answer. Left with little choice in the matter, she moved out of the doorway to make room for him. As he slithered by her, she was pretty sure she saw him wink at her. Then he paused, deliberately and just for a moment, in front of her. With barely any space between them, she was forced to look up. Her breath caught a little as he looked down at her. She had a sudden urge to punch him in that perfect nose.

She made a noncommittal sound and followed them inside. As much as Ava hated to admit it, she was starting to feel hungry. Interviewing useless candidates zapped all her energy, and she couldn't face any more of them today. The takeout smelled amazing, so she opted to focus on that instead.

In the kitchen, Stan grabbed plates for the table as Nick opened the bags of food. Utensils, napkins and containers of food took up the whole surface. She unpacked different kinds of meats, salads, rice and dips. He was right, there was enough food to feed an army, and it smelled like heaven.

"Ava," Stan waved an empty glass at her as he set it down on the table. "Why don't you grab us some beers from the fridge and whatever you're having."

She wasn't picky, and since there was enough beer for all of them, she grabbed three bottles and set them on the table. From her seat, she was able to keep an eye on her grandfather and Nick as they chatted.

"You know, Nick," Stand said with pride. "Ava is a podcaster."

"You don't say," Nick said between bites. "That's really a thing?"

"Imagine that," she said, her eyes blazing at him like a sea during a storm. "So what do you do, Nick? Nick next door."

"I'm a photographer and a videographer," he said evenly. "You know, photoshoots, commercials, videos. Anything that involves a camera. I also have a YouTube channel where I do photography tutorials."

"You're a YouTuber?" she smirked." Is that even a thing?"

"It pays the bills."

Oh, how she wanted to wipe that smug look off his face. She knew men like him. They walked around like they owned the world and expected all women to swoon at their feet. As if. She was sick of slimy guys like him.

Who was he kidding with that scruffy I-just-woke-up-and-got-out-of-shower look? Was this a thing now? He probably spent hours in front of a mirror making sure his hair was perfectly tousled. Also, that designer stubble wasn't fooling anyone.

"You know, Ava," Stan said as he piled more potatoes on his plate. "Nick is quite good. You should check out his work. I think you'd like it."

Ava made a noncommittal sound while she continued to watch Nick as he casually shovelled food in his mouth. She tried to make out the tattoo details that started somewhere under the sleeve of his t-shirt and wound around his arm to his wrist.

"What's with the ink?" she asked.

"Ava," Stan chastised. "Don't be rude to our guest."

"It's fine, Mr. Novak," Nick watched her across the table. When she wasn't busy piling chicken souvlaki on her plate and burying it under a stack of tomatoes, she seemed almost pleasant, less hostile. He lifted the sleeve with his free hand to show her the rest.

"Call it artistic expression," he told her, then glanced at Stan, who winked at him.

Ava wasn't above acknowledging good work when she saw it. Greek warriors, gods and goddesses and mythical beasts set against light bolts, clouds and flowing robes wrapped around his arm. Whoever did the work was very good.

"Were you always such an artistic guy?"

"Not always," he said as he pulled the sleeve down and got back to eating. "I used to have a boring office job that paid the bills."

She let it go as they continued with the meal. Nick seemed totally at ease here, and for some reason, that didn't sit well with her. But she had better things to deal with than an annoying neighbour.

CHAPTER 4

Ava got off the streetcar by the Distillery District and walked over to where Burnett was already waiting for her. Together they walked over to meet with Sam Ellis, the site's supervisor, where Sharon's body was found. The crime scene tape was long gone, but some of the makeshift memorial near the west side of the fence remained.

"People keep leaving stuff there," Sam said when he saw Ava looking in the direction of the memorial. "We tried to leave it there for as long as we could, Miss. But the suits at the HQ were getting antsy, so we took most of it down."

"That's okay," Ava smiled. "I understand. I just didn't expect all these strangers, most of whom never knew her, to show up just like that with flowers and messages."

"It's human nature," Tyler said. "We are all social creatures. There is comfort in uniting with strangers over tragic events, even if there is no connection to the victim. Often it's not so much about the victim but the victim's family. People express their grief and pain more so for the benefit of the family rather than themselves."

"That is true." Sam nodded as he led them inside the gates. "I think the box with all the cards and notes is still in my office," he told her. "We had to dump the flowers, but I can give you the rest if you like."

"That would be great. I appreciate it, Mr. Ellis."

Sam left them to do their thing as he walked back to the trailer to find the box for the daughter. From what he heard on TV, she was just a little kid when the mother went missing. Sometimes life threw some shitty curveballs, he thought, shaking his head.

"Do you think the killer could have been here too?" Ava asked when they were alone. "Maybe he even left something with all the stuff everyone else did?"

"Hard to say," Tyler folded his arms across his chest. "If he or she is still alive and in the area, chances are they were here at some point."

Since the police released the scene, the construction resumed with full force. The area where Sharon's remains were found would soon be dug up to make space for the foundations.

Outside the construction site, life went on as usual. The neighbourhood was busy with cars, pedestrians, dog walkers and people heading to the Distillery District. Couples strolled hand in hand, food delivery couriers zipped by on their bikes with the latest orders, and parents watched their kids play.

The area had a very different vibe in the 1990s when Sharon went missing. What was she doing here?

"The weekend Sharon went missing, she was supposed to meet some friends," he said and gestured west. "There were a few nightclubs not far from here. The friends said they were going to meet her there, but she never showed up. They, the friends, never thought much of it as that wasn't unusual. They assumed something came up."

"She was supposed to come with us to the cottage," Ava said. "I don't remember it, but that's what my grandparents said. She stayed behind, but they didn't know why."

"Perhaps to meet with her killer?" Tyler wondered. "That would mean she knew him or her. Makes sense. Maybe she had something the killer wanted, or they thought she did. She either didn't actually have it or refused to give it up."

That was the sticky point in the whole investigation. After Sharon went missing, over three million dollars disappeared as well. Her employer never filed a report, but the investigation used that as their primary lead. They claimed she embezzled the money over time, and when she had enough, she took off for places unknown.

"That could play with the theory that she found something she wasn't supposed to." Ava's voice interrupted his thoughts.

"Or maybe she wanted something, and the killer wouldn't give it to her," Tyler suggested.

"Like what?"

"Money," he said simply. "Maybe Sharon was blackmailing someone that didn't take kindly to extortion. We shouldn't make the assumption that she found something she was going to expose her killer with. It's possible that she used what she found for blackmail."

Ava didn't like the idea, but it definitely was a possibility. Sharon didn't tell anyone what she found, nor did she express concern over possessing sensitive information. Was she capable of blackmail? That was anyone's guess.

"Did anyone ever find the money?" she said after a few moments. "If she stole money or blackmailed someone, there would be a trail."

"There is always a trail," Tyler said, "but we haven't found it yet. If Sharon was as good as they say she was, she covered her tracks well."

"Do you really think Sharon stole the three million?"

"It doesn't really matter what I think. The facts do. Evidence." Tyler told her truthfully. "Which we have very little of. Today, it's difficult to trace any accounts that far back."

"Did they not do a forensic audit when she went missing?" Ava asked. She was still waiting for copies of the police reports that Burnett promised her.

"It doesn't look like it," he said. "There is no money trail."

"You know, my grandfather believes that she was straight as an arrow," she told him. "According to him, she couldn't have stolen the money. I doubt he'd think she was capable of blackmail."

"I think parents always want to see the best in their children. Do you think he's wrong?" he asked.

"I don't know," she admitted. "But based on what every person has told me about her, Sharon was a meticulous planner. Yet, I haven't found a single piece of evidence or anything she could have hidden. Don't blackmailers keep meticulous records?"

"Makes it easier to keep track if you want to get paid," Tyler said.

***

Ava needed to think. She got dressed, grabbed her headphones and headed outside. The heat hadn't yet set in this early in the morning, so she decided to take full advantage of her run before it got too hot. The streets were quiet, but the neighbourhood was waking up.

People rushed to the subway while others jumped in their cars, trying to beat the traffic. She passed dog walkers, other runners and parents watching over their kids while drinking their morning coffee. The everyday rhythm of the city never really changed that much.

On the Danforth, shopkeepers set up their stores as maintenance crews swept the streets. She passed a delivery truck and turned the music up. Once she made it across the busy street, she increased her pace.

The visit to the site where they found Sharon's remains didn't offer any new clues. She still wasn't totally convinced that Detective Burnett would solve the case, but he seemed solid enough. Ava didn't expect him to agree to her help, but since he did, she now had more information to dig into.

As she ran the parameter of Withrow Park, Ava felt some of the frustration melt away. This case was personal for her, but it didn't mean that she couldn't treat it the same way she did with every other case.

Ava thought of the boxes Sam Elliot gave her and the documents Detective Burnett was sending her way. There was a lot of information to go through. Maybe she really did need an assistant. A fresh set of eyes couldn't hurt either. Unfortunately, she was finding it impossible to find a suitable candidate.

She needed someone right away. It would be great to get someone who had a car and could drive her when she needed to leave town. Maybe she would ask Lori to prioritize applicants who lived in Toronto, or at least somewhere within a short driving distance. Hopefully, they could at least get a temp.

Energized by the newfound clarity, she made her way home just as the heat started to kick in. What she really wanted was a shower, then she would contact Lori about the assistant.

She found Nick lounging casually on the porch steps that connected his parents' house with her grandfather's. Today he wore black shorts and a sleeveless shirt and looked as if just got back from the gym.

Ava rolled her eyes. Over the last few days, she noticed him around. He didn't come over again, but that didn't mean he avoided her. She saw him outside or chatting with her grandfather. Always loitering around. Here was a man with clearly too much time on his hands. Shouldn't he be doing his videos or something?

She accepted his odd friendship with her grandfather, although she was still wary of their connection. As long as he kept her grandfather company, he couldn't be that bad. Stan, after all, had a good head on his shoulders and was no fool when it came to people trying to take advantage of him.

Nick watched her walk up the shared walkway between the houses. She seemed surprised to see him, and in a small way, that gave him some satisfaction. Flushed and sweaty with her hair pulled back in a messy knot, Ava looked as if she had quite the run. She also looked annoyed.

"Good morning," he said casually. "Aren't you a ray of sunshine?"

"It was a good morning," she said pointedly. "Don't you have somewhere to be?"

He smiled. It was one of those arrogant, lazy smiles he undoubtedly used to charm all the women to get what he wanted. She rolled her eyes.

"As it happens, I don't." Nick leaned back against the railing, watching her.

"I guess all those YouTube videos do make themselves."

"You know," he said. "That's the beauty of being your own boss. I happened to do my work in batches, so I don't have to work every day."

"So, you're going to sit here, lounging like a lizard all day?"

"Well, I can think of several things that could keep me busy."

Ava wasn't going to let him bait her. But something clicked.

"I think I'm going to regret this. No, scratch that. I know I will," she said as the idea popped into her head. "Tell me, how are your research skills?"

"Stellar," he told her. "I used to work in marketing. Research was my life. Why?"

"I require a temporary assistant," she said, surprising herself. "Since you seem to be loitering around most of the time, I figure you have time on your hands."

"Maybe, I do."

"It pays," she said. "If you're interested in a temporary gig, that is."

Nick considered her offer. He could use some excitement. "When do I start?"

"Be back here in an hour."

***

Nick was familiar with Stan's house as the layout was almost identical to his parents' house. However, Stan's home was filled with old wooden furniture, travel mementos from various digs he had worked on and lots of pictures. Books were scattered across the house, on shelves, tables and every available surface. The place always reminded him of a den where an old professor, or an adventurer, would have stored all his treasures and memories.

He didn't know why he accepted Ava's offer. He didn't lack for clients, but he was bored. Truth be told, he didn't know anything about true crime podcasts or any podcasts in general. Sharon's disappearance always intrigued him, and he wanted to find out what really happened to her.

Ava's office caught him off guard. A large wooden desk occupied the centre of the room. Three computer screens and a laptop formed a neatly organized row in the middle. Stacks of files occupied every surface of the desk, with pens, pencils and notepads scattered throughout.

There were files in boxes against the wall. And what a wall it was. Ava set up a board with Sharon's pictures, newspaper clippings, timelines and scribbles on sticky notes. It was all meticulously organized and a little disturbing.

"This is some setup," he said as she walked in behind him. "Kinda got that serial killer vibe, don't you think?"

"No, I don't," she said dismissively. "This is where we'll be working, so if that's a problem, you should tell me right now."

This was once Sharon's room. Ava chose it as her office years ago. Over time it was remodelled and updated to suit her needs. It worked because it faced the back of the house and offered a quiet space for her to work. Although she would never admit it, the room helped her feel connected to the woman she barely knew.

"I'm good," he said as he picked up the framed picture of Sharon from the desk. This is exactly how he remembered her. Always smiling. She could make anyone feel as if they were the most important person in the world. "I knew her, you know."

"You did?" she asked.

"Yeah. I would see her around. After you two moved in with your grandparents, she would sometimes come over and talk to my parents. She was always nice to me and the other kids on the street."

Something flashed in her eyes, but it was gone just as fast as it appeared. She looked remarkably like the woman in the picture. It was a bit spooky.

"What exactly do you need me for?" he asked as he set the frame back on the desk. "You didn't exactly give me a job description."

"Make sure you give me your contact info, and I'll send it to Lori, my producer," Ava explained as she pushed a notepad and a pen towards him. "She'll send you the necessary paperwork. As for the job, I need someone to help me with my research, putting the info together, stuff like that."

"Ah, so like a glorified secretary," he said as he wrote down his contact information. "Do you also expect me to get you coffee and make your appointments while I'm at it, too?"

"Very funny," she smirked at him. "I can get my own coffee, thanks. Normally, I would need help researching public records, databases, old files, court documents, and things like that for the cases I'm working on. But right now, I need someone to help me dig through Sharon's case."

She gestured towards the boxes lined up against the wall.

"These are things people left at the makeshift memorial where her remains were found. I'm also waiting for the police reports from the original case and whatever else they have. I need to go through it all, organize and hopefully, find something useful that will tell us who killed her and why."

"I have several upcoming commitments that I need to take care of," Nick said. "They won't take a lot of time, but they need to be done. If you're cool with that, it works for me."

"Great," she said, relieved. "Any other questions?"

"Yeah, there is one thing I'm curious about," he said. "Why do you always refer to her as Sharon? Not mom."

"I don't remember her," she said after a pause. "In so many ways, she's a stranger. I only know her from what others tell me about her."

When Nick didn't say anything, she added, "According to my shrink, it's called compartmentalization. It is how I dealt with the loss and the abandonment issues."

"I'm sorry, that must have been tough," Nick said. He couldn't even fathom what it felt to lose a parent.

"Years of therapy have helped," she said, shrugging her shoulders.

"No doubt," he agreed. "So, where do we start?

***

They sorted through the boxes of cards, poems, and notes left at the site for the next few hours. They organized everything in neat piles with neatly written notes and sorted them alphabetically. Everything was then documented and entered into a spreadsheet that was then saved to the cloud.

As they worked, Ava updated him on the investigation and her meeting with Detective Burnett. She needed Nick to familiarize himself with as many details on the case as possible before the police reports arrived.

"Something about this whole thing still doesn't make sense to me," Ava said between bites when they finally took a break for lunch. They opted for pizza at Nick's suggestion, which significantly raised her opinion of him.

"What's that?"

"Based on everything that I've been told, Sharon was meticulous about keeping records. She kept notes. She was a planner."

"So?"

"So, where did it all go?" she said. "If she was planning to steal three million dollars and disappear, she must have made notes. Plans. She would have developed an escape plan. Written it down somewhere."

Nick considered the question as he ate. "Maybe she hid it somewhere nobody would find it? Or maybe she destroyed everything?"

"I've thought of that," Ava glanced at the wall as she tapped her pencil on the desk. "But how do you steal three million dollars and not leave a trace somewhere? Where is the money?"

"A secret Swiss bank account?"

"I haven't found a trace of one, and neither have the cops." She set the pencil down and crossed her arms. "Clearly, she didn't run away with the money as she's been dead all this time."

"Maybe whoever killed her stole it from her. Or, had her steal it for them and killed her when she handed it over?" Nick suggested.

"I guess everything is possible," she agreed, then added, "Burnett thinks she might have been blackmailing someone."

"I guess that could work too," he agreed. "Blackmail gets tricky, but it's definitely less messy than embezzlement."

"Is it?"

"Well, yeah," Nick said as he wiped the pizza sauce off his hands with a napkin. "Think about it. You find something juicy that someone else doesn't want the world to know. So, you approach them and offer a deal. For the right price, I'll keep what I found to myself. You tell them how much and how often you want them to pay you, and now you've got a nice, steady income stream."

"And what if they don't want to pay?"

"I'd say it depends on the incriminating information," he said. "People are likely to pay up. That's why all these online scams are so popular. You know the ones. You get an email that says someone hacked your computer and will reveal all your secrets to your family and friends. Unless, of course, you pay, preferably in Bitcoin, to make it all go away."

"That's a possibility," she agreed as he laid it out. "Fewer chances of others finding out, and you don't really have to cover any tracks. It's not like the person you're blackmailing is likely to come clean, so nobody else has to know. But, according to my grandfather, Sharon was straight as an arrow."

"Do you always tell your parents everything?" he pointed out. "Everyone has secrets. Maybe she was blackmailing someone. Maybe she did find something she was going to expose. Or, maybe she got mixed up with the wrong people and got in over her head?"

As skeptical as Nick was, he had to consider that maybe Sharon was just that. Honest to a fault. He wasn't exactly the best person to judge a woman he knew briefly as a kid. But if she was innocent, someone made damn sure that she looked guilty.

"I guess Stan knew her better than either one of us, so we could both be wrong." He stared at the wall and the picture of the woman at the centre of it all. "But, what if there never was any money?"

"What do you mean?" she asked.

"The missing money. What if it's just a smokescreen?" he said. "Somebody wanted her gone and made sure she went away. Permanently."

Ava got up from her chair and walked up to the board. She was missing something, and she couldn't put her finger on what it was. The money was always at the centre of Sharon's disappearance, even if there were many unanswered questions about it. It always came down to money.

"If it wasn't about the money," she said, "then what was it about?"

"Something worth killing for."

"Even if there was no money, she was killed because of what she found or had," Ava said as she considered his words. "It still could have been related to blackmail, embezzlement or both."

CHAPTER 5

"How is your new assistant working out?" Lori asked. She was immaculate as always, dressed in a hot pink dress that picked up the colour in the frames of her eyeglasses. Today, her hair was a coil of braids that framed her stunning face to perfection.

"Huh? Oh, Nick," Ava said absently and shrugged. "Adequate."

"That's not a glowing review."

Ava paused for a moment. Nick was surprisingly good at the job. He was thorough, organized and very good at research. They managed to sort through all the documents, conversations with Sharon's friends and coworkers, the newspaper clippings and reports she had collected over the years.

"Okay, maybe adequate doesn't cover it," she said begrudgingly. "So far, he's better than I expected, but that doesn't mean there isn't someone out there who is better."

"He seems nice," Lori said. "Why don't you like him? You hired him, so how bad can he be?"

"I don't know," Ava admitted. "He's got that arrogant smugness about him that annoys me. But, he was close and available. Plus, my grandfather likes him. He'll do for now."

"Right," Lori nodded. "I look forward to meeting him then."

"Can we get back to business now?"

They went over the numbers of the new season of The Missing Voices. The downloads and subscriptions were up, and so were the revenues. That made everyone happy, especially since true crime podcasting was a very saturated area. Ava's show had a solid listener base before she joined forces with Odyssey. Still, the extra resources helped drive engagement across social platforms and spread the word.

When Ava ran The Missing Voices on her own, she averaged between six to ten episodes a season, with two seasons each year. Each episode took about thirty hours to produce, which often took up more time than she wanted. When Lori's company took on the production, they increased the number of episodes to fifteen. Now that a team took on most of the behind-the-scenes work, Ava could do what she did best, tell stories of those that no longer have a voice, and promote the podcast.

"Since you're in Toronto," Lori said. "How do you feel about doing an event there to promote the show? You know, the group you've met with in the past?"

"I think that can be arranged."

"Great. The team is still sorting through all the emails from listeners and forwarding you the important ones," Lori said. They received thousands of emails from listeners, ranging from tips related to the featured cases and theories to fan mail. "We have also narrowed down a list of cases for the next season based on your notes," Lori continued. "Once we have that finalized, I'll get the preliminary research started."

More listeners also meant more requests to find missing loved ones. While Ava wanted to help them all, it was impossible to cover every single case. Having a team to sort through all the requests made the process more efficient and guaranteed to keep them busy for years.

Ava cross-checked her own notes and confirmed tentative dates.

"I'd like to tackle them based on location," Ava said. "There are a few in Colorado and a few others on this side of the border in Alberta. It would be easier to get all the info all at once instead of flying back and forth."

"I don't think that will be a problem," Lori agreed and made some notes herself. "Do you have any preferences for where you want to go first?"

"Not really," Ava said. "I can go to either one. Maybe once we have an idea of what information is available, it'll be easier to narrow down. Meanwhile, I'll keep you posted about the event."

"Sounds good, Ava. I'll be in touch."

Ava reached out to the event organizer and copied Nick on all the correspondence. She followed up with several leads and made several inquiries about Sharon's case. As per his word, Detective Burnett provided copies of reports on her mother's case, including those from the original investigation.

Burnett also provided contact information for the former investigator, Frank Mitchell. Without wasting any time, Ava picked up the phone and called him. He didn't pick up, so she left her name and contact information, asking him to get back to her. Until she heard back, she was going to get more acquainted with Frank.

***

"So, explain this to me again," Nick said as he drove. "Why don't you have a driver's license?"

"I never needed one," Ava said. She didn't have to explain herself to him.

Nick looked over at her with a dubious look on his face. "You never needed one? How do you get around?"

"I grew up in Toronto and London. Both cities have transportation infrastructure that makes it easy to get around," she said. "Why would I need a car?"

"Having a car and knowing how to drive are two different things."

"I know how to drive," she told him defensively.

"Then why don't you have a driver's licence? Surely, you've been to places where there are no subways, busses and streetcars. How do you get around then?"

"By hiring drivers," she said impatiently. "Ones that don't ask a million questions that are none of their concern."

"Whatever you say, boss," he laughed. She clearly lacked a sense of humour. "So, what's the story with this guy we're going to see?"

Ava opened the file on her lap and flipped through the information she printed out earlier.

"Frank Mitchell," she said. "The original investigator on Sharon's case. His notes on the investigation are pretty sketchy. According to what he wrote, nothing in Sharon's life indicated that she was involved in something shady. Family and friends didn't see any changes in her behaviour. Nor did she confide in any of them about anything that worried her."

"Is that it?" Nick asked. "There has to be more."

"Well, he does mention something about the money, but it's more of a side note."

"Did he do any actual investigating?"

"Depends on how you look at it," she said. "I don't think he put a lot of effort into narrowing down exactly when Sharon disappeared. My grandparents filed a report after we got back from the cottage. That's only a few days, let's say three or four, during which she could have gone missing."

"Did he ever consider that something could have happened to her?

"That's definitely something I want to ask him," Ava said. "But according to my grandfather, he didn't spend too much time chasing any other angles."

"This whole case doesn't really make sense. A woman goes missing, and they don't automatically think that something might have happened to her? Where does the money fit in?"

"All good questions," Ava agreed. "Again, not something I can answer. Burnett made some notes here. Essentially what he says is that Walker, Sharon's boss, never filed any reports about missing money. Burnett couldn't find any information indicating that Mitchell had a forensic investigation done on Sharon's office computer, her bank accounts or the company's. No trace of the money that supposedly went missing with the woman who masterminded the whole operation."

They drove in silence. Sharon's case, seemingly open and shut, proved to be anything but. It was built solely on the assumption that she stole the money and fled. Yet, there was no money trail.

"That's a pretty huge leap," Nick said as he navigated the road. "From a missing woman to three million dollars that may or may not have been missing with her. How do they even put the two together?"

"I think there was a note somewhere in here," Ava said as she searched for the page, she had in mind. "The only evidence of money is a short statement from the bookkeeper, Debbie Styles. Styles claimed that small sums of money were siphoned from the gallery's accounts over time, to a tune of just over three million."

"What does that have to do with Sharon?"

"She was the one in charge of the accounts. Accounts payable, receivables, fundraising. Things like that."

"Still, that's a far stretch. Where did the money go then?"

"Good question," Ava agreed. "According to Mitchell, Sharon was a computer hacker. Did they even have hackers back then? Anyway, he claims she had access to the money and knew how to hide it. Apparently, in his world, you don't need actual facts. Just enough to pick and choose to fit the narrative that works best."

It took them over two hours to reach Frank Mitchell's house. She didn't expect to find the former Toronto cop living in a small town. It was definitely a change of pace, and maybe that's what he was looking for in his retirement. Somehow, Mitchell didn't strike her as the outdoorsy type.

Curious, she examined the house before she got out of the car. Mitchell lived in a cottage-style back split bungalow that sat on several acres of land. It was surrounded by pine and cedar trees. The house had a wrap-around porch that overlooked the lake and a boathouse.

"Nice place," Nick said as he looked around. "Shall we?"

***

Mitchell watched the red Jeep pull up in front of his house and waited for his visitors to get out. He was a tall, burly man with a round face, white beard and a balding head. He might have been retired, but his eyes were all cop.

"You must be Ava Reed," he said.

"And that would make you Frank Mitchell," Ava said with a smile. "This is my associate, Nick."

"Nice to meet you both. Call me Frank."

They followed him inside. The house was furnished comfortably with a newly renovated kitchen and a massive TV in the living area. There were family pictures scattered around the house on walls and on most available surfaces. Several art pieces decorated the walls, fitted neatly in between the family photos.

"The wife is out shopping, so we can take this outside on the porch. Enjoy the views and all that." Frank opened the fridge and took out a beer. "Can I get you anything?"

"We're good," Ava told him. "We don't want to take too much of your time."

"Suit yourself," Frank opened the beer, took a swig and motioned for them to follow him outside.

"How are you enjoying retirement?" Ava asked once they were seated outside.

"Retirement can get overrated. I miss being a cop sometimes," he said as he slumped into one of the patio chairs outside. "Chasing leads, catching the bad guys. The thrill of busting up drug rings and getting killers off the streets."

Ava and Nick exchanged amused glances. If he was more diligent about chasing leads when Sharon went missing, maybe he would have solved it sooner.

"That's why we're here, Frank," Ava said. "As I explained on the phone, Sharon Novak was my mother. I was hoping that maybe you had some insights you could share with me about her case."

"Sharon Novak," Mitchell said. "That takes me back some. Never thought they would find her dead."

He drank some more beer as he stared out at the lake. "You look a lot like her," he said, turning his attention to Ava.

"Yes, I've been told. Like I mentioned on the phone, I have a podcast about finding missing people," Ava said, looking him straight in the eye. "I want to do a series that focuses on my mother's case and the investigation."

"Not sure I can tell you anything that's not in the files," he said. His gaze went back to the water.

"Did you ever consider that she could be dead?" Ava asked. "When she first went missing, I mean?"

"Didn't seem like it. All signs pointed to her stealing the money and taking off. I figured she took off for a better life."

"But you never found the money trail?"

"She was that good. Skimmed money bit by bit over time, and nobody knew a thing until she went missing."

Ava had her own opinion but kept it to herself for now.

"There is nothing in these reports about the money," she said. "No traces on accounts, nothing on Adam Walker filing a report about the missing money. Who reported it gone."

"Walker never filed an official report," Frank said. "You know how it is with rich people. They don't want the scandal or can't admit that someone on staff embezzled from them. Since the money was discovered after she went missing, we didn't file charges."

"But someone must have noticed it gone in the first place?"

Frank drank his beer. When he realized the bottle was empty, he grabbed another from the cooler beside him and opened it. He chugged it like it was water.

"I think someone found discrepancies in the accounts after Sharon disappeared," he tried to remember the name. "The bookkeeper, some woman. I can't remember her name."

"Did you find anything when you searched her house? Office?"

"We searched her parents' house. Her place of residence. We checked the ex's house. I guess that's your father's place," he motioned to Ava, and she nodded. "Nada. We checked the borders, airports and train stations, but she had a few days on us. With that kind of money, she most likely got a fake ID, and we lost the trail."

"Was there anyone in her life at the time that could have killed her and took the money?" Ava asked.

"That is the question for the ages," Mitchell set down the now empty bottle and reached for another one. "There were plenty of guys hanging around her back then. She was a looker, your mother."

"Now that we know she's dead," Ava continued, ignoring the comment. "Any idea as to who might have killed her?"

"None," Frank said without giving it much thought. "I'm sorry to say this, but she likely went to a bad part of town, and someone decided she didn't belong. Pretty straightforward."

It was too easy of an answer, but it didn't seem like they would get much more out of Mitchell. They said their goodbyes and got back in the car.

***

Nick glanced in his rearview mirror as Frank Mitchell watched them drive away. He stood there, unsmiling, and when the red Jeep finally disappeared from view, he reached for his phone and made a call.

"What did you think of Mitchell?" Nick asked.

"I think my grandfather was right. He didn't really care as to what happened to Sharon," she said. "I'm surprised he agreed to meet with us in the first place."

"Why is that?"

"He wasn't very forthcoming when I spoke to him," she shrugged. "I think he took offence to having his investigation under scrutiny."

"I think he knows more than he's saying," Nick said. "He was watching us leave. If he didn't care about the case or didn't know something, he wouldn't have bothered."

Ava looked out the window at the passing scenery. She had a feeling Frank Mitchell knew a lot more than he was saying. The question was why.

"How much do you think that place is worth?" she asked.

"Depends," Nick thought about it. "I'd say in the one to two million dollars range?"

"Interesting isn't it." She mused. "How does a mid-level, average cop afford a house like that?"

"He could have sold his house in Toronto and took the profit to buy this one," Nick said as he turned into the road that led to the nearest small town. "We can check when he bought it and for how much. Meanwhile, why don't we grab some lunch? I'm starving."

They pulled into a parking lot of a cute restaurant they spotted off the road. It had a lovely patio filled with flowerpots and string lights. They chose a table in the shade facing the street. Ava opted for fish and chips while Nick went with a burger and fries. The service was fast, and the food smelled delicious.

"What's next?" Nick asked between bites.

"I want to talk to Burnett again," Ava said as she cut into her fish. "He might have some insights into Mitchell. Plus, we still have all those police reports to go through."

"Are you going to talk about Sharon's case at the meetup?"

"Probably not. I don't want to take away from the cases we feature this season. Sharon's case is still open, and there isn't much to add."

"Maybe not yet," he said as a black pickup truck tailed it out of the parking lot behind the building. They watched as it disappeared in the distance. "Someone's in a hurry."

They finished their meal, enjoying a civil conversation. When he wasn't trying so hard, Nick wasn't totally annoying. She could see what her grandfather saw in him.

"All right," she said as she wiped her hands. "I'll pay up, and we should hit the road again."

"You're the boss," Nick said as he winked at her.

Ava paid the bill and went to meet Nick in the parking lot. Even from a short distance, she could see that something was wrong.

"What happened?" she asked.

"Looks like someone wanted to send us a message," Nick said and pointed at his slashed tire. "They also left a note."

She was going to say something about preserving the fingerprints when he reached into the car and produced a clear bag. The note was carefully placed inside it.

"'Stop looking and don't come back,'" she read. "What does that mean?"

"Looks like someone didn't like us going around and asking questions," Nick said as he scanned the parking lot. No security cameras or witnesses. "I'd say Frank definitely knows something he's not saying."

"Do you think it was someone in the black pickup truck?"

"Possibly," Nick said as he went to take the spare tire off the back of his Jeep. "I'd say it was a warning. If they were more serious, they would have slashed all our tires."

"Makes sense," she nodded. "Slashing a tire is more of an inconvenience. Slashing them all would force us to stay here and ask more questions. Whoever did this didn't want us sticking around."

It didn't take long to change the tire and mount the slashed one in the back. Since they didn't think the local cops could do much, they packed it up and headed back to Toronto. As they drove, Ava emailed Burnett pictures of the slashed tire and the note. She also included a brief update on their visit and asked to meet with the detective again.

The rest of the drive home was uneventful, but they both kept an eye out on anyone that might be following them or paying too much attention. Whoever wanted them gone meant business.

CHAPTER 6

Like so many homes in neighbourhoods across Toronto, the Laskaris and Novak properties had small structures built behind their backyards facing the alley. While some homeowners converted theirs into laneway houses, others still used theirs for storage.

Nick and Stan stood side by side in the alley behind their properties. Neither one could pass as a functioning garage anymore, but they weren't in any usable shape either.

"The way I look at it," Nick said as he rubbed his chin, "we either tear down the whole thing, or we try to salvage what we can."

Stan tugged at the door on his side, trying to pry it open without success.

"I don't think we can do much with this one," he said. "I haven't had much use for a garage since I stopped driving."

"Let me try, Mr. Novak," he said.

"Oh, Nick," Stan moved out of his way. "I told you to call me Stan."

Nick grinned at him as he tugged at the door. After a few tries, it finally budged enough for him to open it. They both stared at the mess inside.

"When exactly did you stop driving, Stan?" he asked. "Last century?"

The garage was filled with what seemed like random household items, boxes and gardening tools. Everything was covered in dust and cobwebs.

"It's like a time capsule in here," Nick said in amazement.

"I honestly can't remember the last time I was in here," Stan said with surprise as he poked his head inside. "I doubt there is anything of value here. My wife used it for storage."

It would take a few sessions to sort through this. Nick suspected Stan would enjoy rummaging through it all.

"How about we see what's on the other side?" Nick suggested.

"Somehow, I don't see your parents as pack rats," Stan smiled. "But, at this rate, nothing will surprise me anymore."

They moved to Nick's parents' side of the garage. While it was also in a terrible shape, the door sported a newer lock. Without the need to tug at the door, Nick fished the key out of his pocket and unlocked it. It opened with ease. The two stared at the empty space.

"How about that?" Stan nudged Nick as he smiled. "Told you they weren't packrats."

Nick walked into the vacant space. It was larger than he remembered and offered more possibilities than he imagined.

"How about that," he said. "I should move my Jeep in here."

"I heard about what happened yesterday," Stan said. "Do you think someone might try to damage your car again?

"You never know," Nick said. "Digging in the past can bring up a lot of memories. Some people might not want that."

Stan nodded as if agreeing with him.

"I do worry about Ava sometimes," he said. "She has a way of digging for things that might make people nervous."

"What do you mean?" Nick asked. "Has anyone threatened her in the past over any of the cases?"

"I think occasionally she gets emails or messages from really nasty people," Stan said as he watched Nick lock up the door of his parent's garage. "She doesn't want me to worry, but I do overhear her sometimes when she talks with that producer of hers. I think they now screen a lot of her messages to weed out the crazies. Still, I worry about her."

They made their way back to the street. It was a nice day, so Stan invited Nick for a drink. They sat on the porch when Stan gestured at the house with his glass of wine.

"I'm actually thinking of selling the house," he said. "I'm getting too old to maintain it by myself."

"Have you told Ava?" Nick asked. He didn't think she would be happy about that decision.

"Not yet," Stan sighed. "I've always hoped that one day Sharon would come back, so I stayed here because I didn't want her to think that we moved away. It sounds foolish when I say it out loud."

"I don't think it's foolish," Nick said. "It's very thoughtful, actually."

"Now that I know she's not coming back, there is no reason to stay," he said. "Too many memories locked in here anyway. Don't say anything to her."

"Don't worry, I won't."

Ava found them still sitting on the porch when she got home from the gym. She was tired and sweaty and in need of a shower. But they looked so comfortable, so she decided to join them for a bit.

"Did you have a good workout, dear?" Stan asked.

"Sure did, Grandpa," she beamed at him. "What are you smirking at?" she said to Nick.

"Smirking?" he said, rolling his eyes. "I'm sorry, but I don't see yoga as that much of a workout."

"Don't knock it till you try it," she said, narrowing her eyes. "Yoga is a great way to work the muscles and does wonders for flexibility. But if you must know, today I had a kickboxing class."

"Well, look at you. What are you, Rocky, now?"

"You laugh now, "she said as she got up. "But you'll be crying when I kick your ass."

His laughter followed her all the way inside. Jerk, she thought.

***

Tyler arrived at the sleek offices of the NorFast Group a few minutes early. He finally managed to get a meeting with Elizabeth Northam, despite trying several times. Even though he had an appointment, he was forced to wait in the lobby. It was a large space decorated with gold accents and modern furniture. There were no sounds other than the receptionist occasionally answering the phone in hushed tones. For a large office, it was strangely quiet.

He rechecked his watch – he's been sitting in the lobby for over half an hour. He usually didn't let things get a rise out of him, but he recognized a power play when he saw one. Elizabeth Northam made sure that he knew who was in charge here.

Unfazed, he picked up the glass of water the receptionist offered him upon arrival. He took a sip and set it back down. He then pulled out his notebook from his jacket pocket and flipped through the notes one more time. His thoughts were interrupted by the receptionist, who then ushered him into Elizabeth's office.

She sat behind a massive desk and didn't get up when Tyler entered the office. She motioned for him to sit down in one of the chairs facing the desk. She wore a sleek, red power suit and a look of annoyance. She folded her hands neatly in front of her and smiled politely.

"Detective Burnett," she said. "I'm sorry to keep you waiting."

Since she sounded anything but, Tyler returned the bland smile with one of his own as he sat down.

"Thank you for seeing me," he said. "I know you're busy, so I won't take up a lot of your time."

Elizabeth continued to smile politely, but the smile never reached her eyes. She nodded for him to continue as if she couldn't wait to get this meeting over with.

"Like I told your assistant," Tyler began. "I'm investigating the death of Sharon Novak. The woman whose remains were found at your construction site," he clarified when she didn't acknowledge the name.

"It was an unfortunate event," she said. "But I'm not sure what this has to do with me."

"The discovery of human remains gotta be bad for business."

"That is why we have things like insurance, Detective," she said. "It's a minor inconvenience."

"You don't think people might object to living where human remains were found?'

"Not to sound insensitive, but we're not talking about a cemetery here," she pointed out. "We are talking about a prime downtown location in a vibrant and in-demand city. There is no shortage of people willing to overlook a minor inconvenience so they can own a piece of real estate in Toronto."

"Did you know the deceased?" he asked, switching gears.

One of Elizabeth's eyebrows shot up in question. She angled her head slightly without breaking eye contact.

"Should I?"

"Sharon Novak was employed by your brother, Adam Walker, at the time of her disappearance."

"Adam is my step-brother, Detective," she said smoothly. "I'm afraid that we're not very close. I don't get involved in his affairs, and he doesn't get involved in mine. You can't expect me to know every single person in his employ, especially over two decades ago."

"Surely you recognize the name? It was all over the news when she went missing," Tyler said as he watched her. "It was in the news again when her remains were found on your construction site."

"Of course, I recognize the name," she said impatiently. "You asked if I knew her."

"And you didn't?"

"Not that I recall."

Tyler went back to his notebook and slowly flipped through the pages. She watched him silently.

"What do you think happened to the money?" he asked suddenly.

"I beg your pardon?"

"The money," he said again. "The three million dollars that went missing from your brother's company. The money Sharon Novak was accused of stealing."

"How should I know, Detective Burnett?" she asked, but there was a bit of an edge in her voice this time.

"Mr. Walker never filed a police report. You'd think that with such a large amount of money missing, he would want it back," he paused. "Embezzlement is a crime. He could have filed charges against Sharon Novak."

Elizabeth watched him carefully. Her perfectly made-up face devoid of any sort of emotion. Tyler could sense that she did not appreciate his line of questioning.

"I'm afraid that I can't answer that," she said flatly. "I don't get involved in my brother's business affairs. You'd have to ask him."

"Any idea where I can find him?" he asked.

"No," she said firmly. "Is there anything else?"

"Not at this time. You've been very accommodating," Tyler said as he got up. "Thank you for your time, Ms Northam. I'll show myself out."

Elizabeth watched him leave without a word. When he stopped at the door and turned to her, he saw another flash of anger, but it quickly disappeared.

"Just one more question," he said. "When did your company acquire the Silver Clover property?"

"My family has owned the property for quite some time," she said. "I'm sure someone on my staff can get you that detail. Now, if you excuse me, I have a meeting that I have to attend."

Tyler nodded in acknowledgement and left. He could feel her piercing gaze following him as he walked away. It seems like he ruffled some feathers in Elizabeth's perfect life. He got on the elevator and stood silently in the back as people filed in and out on different floors. Delivery people, suits running to meetings and interns snickering at their supervisors. The corporate world never lacked entertainment.

He thought about Sharon Novak. He didn't expect it to be easy when he took on this case, but the more he dug, the more curious he became. Nobody seemed to know anything. There was no evidence of any crime and no trace of Sharon or the money. Everything was very neat. A bit too neat, he thought.

When he got to the station, Tyler found Ava waiting for him.

***

"Hello, Detective," she said with a smile.

"You should call me Tyler," he said. "What can I do for you?"

"I wanted to thank you again for sending me the police reports," Ava said. "It's helpful to understand what was happening with the investigation when Sharon went missing."

"It's the least I can do," he said. "As you have noticed, there is not a lot of information in those files. At least not as much as I would have expected."

"You mean this is not the standard way to collect information during an investigation?" she asked with a raised eyebrow. She tried to keep the sarcasm to a minimum, but sometimes it took better of her.

Tyler smiled, let the comment pass.

"It sounds like you had quite the day visiting Frank Mitchell," Tyler pulled up the pictures she sent him on his computer screen. "Did you bring the note with you?"

She dug the clear plastic baggie out of her purse and handed it over.

"I don't know what you can do with this, but maybe you can get something useful off the note."

Tyler examined the note. The message, printed in block letters using a marker, was pretty clear in its meaning.

"Looks like your visit stirred some resentment," he said.

"I don't know if it was Mitchell who wrote the note and left it, or someone else was there watching the house."

"If Frank was the one who wrote it or touched it at any time, his fingerprints would be on the paper," he told her. "His are in the system, so we'll know soon enough if he was behind it."

She told him about the black pickup truck that tore out of the parking lot while they were having lunch.

"Unfortunately, we didn't get the plates."

"Well, you couldn't have known. Besides," Tyler pointed out. "It might have been someone else, not connected to the truck."

"You're right," she sighed. "We didn't notice any vehicle matching the truck when we went to see Mitchell, so we didn't think it was connected. Besides, I doubt Mitchell would be able to drive."

"Why is that?"

"Well," she hesitated. "I'm pretty sure he's a heavy drinker. He had three beers just in the short time we were there. He might have had more before we got there."

"I see," Tyler knew from experience that drinking hasn't stopped many people from getting behind the wheel. Still, he didn't know Mitchell enough to tell whether Frank was one of those people or not. "Let me talk to him and see what shakes out."

"Do you think he'll tell you more than he told us?"

"It's worth a try."

"You should keep an eye out for any black pickup trucks while you're there," she said.

"I will. Meanwhile," Tyler said as he opened a drawer in his desk. "Do you know if Sharon had any safety deposit boxes, lockers or storage rooms?"

"Not that I am aware," Ave thought about the possibility. "If she did, she didn't tell anyone."

Tyler pulled out an evidence bag. Inside was a small key. He handed the bag to Ava.

"What's this?" she asked.

"I was hoping you could tell me," he said. "This was found with Sharon's remains. It's unclear if it belonged to her or to her killer."

"I can ask my grandfather and my father if they know anything," she offered as she examined the key. "But I seriously doubt it. If she has anything like that, I'm sure someone would have contacted either one of them to ask for payment."

"Well, it was worth a try," Tyler said and put the evidence bag back in the drawer. "I'll keep looking."

"Have you talked to Sharon's old boss yet?" Ava asked.

"No," Tyler said as he crossed his arms. "I'm still looking for him."

"Maybe that's something I can look into."

***

Ava checked her watch. She had a few more minutes to spare before her next meeting. She made her way down Broadview Avenue towards the coffee shop where she was set to meet Kevin Smith, the man behind the meetup group and the true crime community in Toronto.

Since she was early, Ava grabbed a coffee and snagged a newly vacated table outside. It was a lovely day to sit outside without the stifling humidity. No interruptions, no expectations. Ava enjoyed moments like this when she could just sit and observe the world around her.

"Ava?"

She looked up at the sound of her name and waved to Kevin. He made his way over to where she sat and gave her a quick hug. He had a square jaw, shaggy blond hair and the look of a perpetual student.

"So good to see you again, Ava," he said as he sat his saddlebag on one of the chairs. "I hope you haven't been waiting long."

"Oh, no," she told him. "I got here early and thought I'd enjoy the view."

"Can't blame you," he smiled. "I'm going to grab a coffee. Do you want anything else?"

She shook her head and watched him go inside. Kevin was one of the true crime podcast fans she had met years ago. He was actively involved with the online community in Toronto. He organized many of any meetups or events she spoke at. He was also a huge supporter of her podcast and a great outlet to promote the new season of The Missing Voices.

"Tell me everything," he said dramatically once he sat down again. "What's new and exciting? How is the new season going?"

She laughed. Kevin was always so eager to help. He was intelligent, easy to talk to, and had connections to the local true crime community she needed. Ava also suspected he had a little crush on her. Thankfully, their relationship always stayed professional.

She filled him in on the feedback on the latest season, the cases she wanted to highlight and how Lori's idea for a meetup came about. Kevin was on board and loved everything about it. That's what Ava liked about him. He was easygoing and got things done.

They have done events together in the past, and they have always sold out. You could say that people couldn't get enough of death and murder. It always amazed her just how many people listened to her podcast. She often got emails from strangers telling her how the stories affected them. Most of them expressed sympathies for the families, others offered theories and, every now and then, someone actually had information related to a case. Those emails came less often and even fewer led to solving the cases. But those that did made all her work worthwhile. Especially if they lead to a break in an investigation.

"This is great," Kevin said as he wrote down the details. "I think we can organize something next week. Would that be too soon?"

"You think you can get it done in time?"

"I don't see why not. We already had a tentative date set, and it was one of those that worked for Lori. Besides," he smiled at her. "The people love you. I" m sure they'll be eager to come out and hear you speak."

"You're too kind."

"I speak the truth," he said, then snapped his notebook shut. "Now, tell me, what's new with your mom's case. I didn't see you post any updates online."

Ava sipped the rest of her coffee. She hadn't posted anything about Sharon since they found her remains. There just wasn't much to say. She had Nick sort through the comments and messages on the site to see if anyone left anything useful. So far, there was nothing.

"There is no news to share," she told him truthfully. "I'm actually doing some research work on the original case, trying to find something useful."

"Are you treating it like one of the other cases?"

"Yes," she nodded. "I decided to dig deeper. I have an assistant who is helping me sort through everything. Two sets of eyes should be better than one."

"Oh definitely. I didn't know you were looking for an assistant.," he pouted. "I would have totally loved to apply."

"You're already busy," she said. "But I totally appreciate it."

"Do the police have any leads?" Kevin asked.

"Nothing concrete," Ave said. She definitely wasn't going to admit that her mother could have been a blackmailer. It was already bad enough that people thought she embezzled money. "I am working on some angles, but as you can appreciate, I can't share them right now."

"Of course," he patted her hand. "I am here if you need me. Don't hesitate to call if you need anything. Or, if the assistant doesn't work out."

CHAPTER 7

Ava started the day with a workout. While kicking, punching, lifting and stretching helped relieve some of the frustration, she was still left with more questions than answers. She didn't like to think her mother was capable of blackmail any more than being a thief. Unfortunately, many things were pointing that way.

Maybe she needed to talk to someone whose opinion of Sharon was less rosy. Someone who didn't just see the positive. Her father. Ava checked her watch and decided to call London.

Michael answered after several rings, and his face filled the screen. Ava knew her father wasn't too keen on talking about Sharon, but she had to try since he could provide some answers. They exchanged the usual pleasantries before she got down to business.

"I have some questions about Sharon," she said.

"I don't know what I can tell you that you don't already know," he sighed. "You have let it go, Ava. I know she was your mother, but she didn't run away. You don't have to chase her anymore."

She hated bringing Sharon up. He always looked pained when talking about her mother. He avoided the topic whenever he could, even with Stan.

"Someone killed her, Dad. I want to know why."

Michael pressed his fingers to his temples. Massaged them out of a habit. He could feel throbbing pain coming on somewhere inside his head. Even in death, Sharon's grip was strong and vengeful.

"Ava," he said slowly. "Sharon was a complicated person. She did everything her way and didn't listen to reason. She was only concerned with what was best for Sharon. That's it. Many people didn't take kindly to that."

"Do you think she was capable of blackmailing someone?"

Something passed across Michael's face, but he didn't immediately respond. She could sense tension and anger but didn't know why.

"Sharon liked to stick her nose in other people's business," he said. "Not everyone appreciated that."

"What does that mean?"

"It means your mother wasn't the selfless do-gooder your grandfather makes her out to be. He's put her on a pedestal, for god's sake, like some sort of a martyr. She was far from perfect. She knew how to get to people, exploit them," he paused as if trying to control the anger. "Blackmail? I wouldn't put it past her."

"That doesn't mean she deserved to die," Ava said quietly.

"No, of course not. That's not what I'm saying."

"What are you saying, Dad?"

He exhaled in frustration. He was so sick and tired of having to deal with Sharon Novak. The woman was a thorn in his side. One he couldn't get rid of no matter how much he tried.

"Look, she was your mother," he said. "No matter how I felt about her, I know she loved you very much. When she disappeared, I was so angry with her. Angry with her for leaving you."

"Did you think she left on purpose?"

Michal shrugged. "I don't know. A part of me thought that maybe she did, and I hated her for it. But in a way, I was glad she was out of my life," he admitted. "I'm sorry, Ava. I truly am. I'm sorry you didn't get to know her. I'm sorry she is dead because that means she's not coming back."

"But you're not sorry she is gone."

When he didn't answer, she just stared, unsure how to respond. Ava never doubted that her father loved her. Growing up, he was always there for her, making sure she had everything she needed. He paid for horseback riding lessons, summer camps, private schools and shrinks without a single complaint. He sent her to spend summers with her grandparents and never complained if they wanted her to come any other time.

She always thought it was to fill the void left by Sharon's disappearance, maybe even guilt. Now, she wasn't sure. Maybe he sent her away so she wouldn't remind him of Sharon. A painful reminder of the woman he couldn't stand to be around. Did he ever love her?

"Did you talk to her before she went missing?" she asked.

"Sharon didn't fill me in on the details in her life. We were barely speaking to each other, except when it came to you."

"So you don't know if she was seeing anyone or if anyone was bothering her?"

"No. Sharon could be very secretive when she wanted to be. There were always men hanging around her. She could have been seeing any one of them, but she never told me about anyone."

"When did you see her last?"

"It was a few days before she went missing. I dropped you off at your grandparents', and we had some words, then I went straight to the airport."

Ave couldn't tell if he genuinely didn't know anything else or just didn't care.

"You should let it go," he said and raised his hand when she was about to protest. "The truth, or whatever version of it you get, is not going to bring her back. You were looking for her for years, and now you've found her. Take that and move on. She's not coming back."

After the call ended, Ava shut the laptop in frustration.

***

It was always the same old thing. Ava thought as she paced around her office. To many, Sharon was a brilliant, charming and attractive woman with so much potential. To others, she was a persistent, self-righteous, pushy and scheming busybody. Was she all of it, or was she none of those things?

"Ugh," Ava whipped the stress ball she's been squeezing against the wall. "Sharon, Sharon, SHARON."

"Tough morning?" Tyler asked. He leaned lazily against the doorway, watching the stress ball bounce off the wall and roll on the floor.

He caught her off guard. Ava stared at him, her eyes blazing.

"I see you finally decided to show up," she said. "Wild party last night?"

"No party," he grinned. "I had a date. It ended late."

He lifted the small paper bag he was holding to show her. "And before you get all twisted out of shape, I brought you coffee."

She accepted the coffee cup begrudgingly and let it go. It wasn't his fault she didn't remember her own mother and had to rely on the opinion of others to understand her.

"What do we work on today? he asked.

"I went to see Tyler, I mean Detective Burnett," Ava said. "I gave him the note."

"So it's Tyler now," he teased, giving her a knowing look. "I see."

"Get your mind out of the gutter," she said. "We need to do some digging into Sharon's old boss. Adam Walker. Burnett can't locate him."

"Well, then. Good thing for my superior research skills."

"You found him?" she asked.

"Not yet, but I did some digging into his family history," Nick said as he sat at the desk and opened his laptop. "You might find it interesting to know that the property where Sharon's remains were found belongs to a company owned by Elizabeth Northam."

"Who's she?"

"I'm glad you asked," Nick continued as he opened his notes. "Elizabeth and Adam are related."

"What?" Ava asked as she leaned over his shoulder to take a better look at the screen. "How?"

"The short version is that her father, George Elliot Northam, married his mother, Teresa Walker," Nick said as he tried to ignore her hair ticking his face. But she made no attempt to move.

"That's it?" she asked. "Did you find anything useful about the family?"

"Oh, ye of little faith," he said and moved her hair out of the way. She moved back then decided to sit on the edge of the desk as he pulled up the information." George, the patriarch of the Northam family, was the only child born to Mary and Henry Northam during the Great Depression.

"His family made their money in shipping at the turn of the century and did quite well for the first two decades. When the Depression hit, Henry's entrepreneurial spirit kicked in, and he started to resell the goods he couldn't ship anymore from a storefront."

"Nicely done. What else?"

"Well, Henry then invested his profits into real estate, buying up properties at rock bottom prices. George, Elizabeth's father, continued the family tradition," Nick told her. "By the early 1970s, he amassed quite a portfolio. He owned several large parking lots in strategic parts of the city. They were eventually developed or sold off for a tidy profit that increased the family coffers. After trying his hand at development, George started the NorFast Group, the company his daughter Elizabeth is now in charge of."

"Interesting," Ava said. "When did he marry Adams' mother?"

"Well, George had three wives," Nick leaned back in his chair as he continued to read the info. "His first marriage ended in annulment, and not much info is available on the first Mrs. Northam. Wife number two, Victoria, gave him one daughter, Elizabeth. Victoria died in a car accident, and George married his third wife, Teresa, shortly after. He adopted her son, Adam, who at the time was almost eighteen."

"Why adopt him?" Ava wondered. "I mean, adult adoptions are not unheard of, but they are less common." She leaned in to look at the screen. "It says here that the adoption was approved almost immediately after the wedding took place. Weird."

"Well, that's one way of procuring yourself a son," Nick pointed out. When she gave him a look, he said, "Hey, I'm not against daughters, but some dudes, especially the old school ones, are all about that male heir."

"Hmmm, I wonder how Elizabeth felt about the wedding and the adoption," Ava wondered. "You get a brand new mommy and a brother all in one."

"Interestingly enough," Nick pointed out, "Adam didn't take on his stepfather's name."

"What do we know about him?"

"He has a degree in fine arts. This is probably why he ran the gallery where Sharon worked. He went into politics after the gallery closed in the late 1990s."

They studied Adam's images on the screen. He was an attractive man with an air of importance. The charming smile made him appear approachable. He was well-liked, although his image leaned more towards a party-boy persona than a seasoned politician.

Adam Walker left politics suddenly after an unsuccessful run for the mayor's office several years ago. There wasn't much in the news about him after that. While many politicians often shifted into consulting in the private sector or academia after giving up their political careers, there was nothing on record for Walker.

"We need to find him."

***

After days of digging relentlessly through files, reports and evidence, exhaustion started to set in. When Nick suggested they head out for a drink, she reluctantly agreed. One drink couldn't hurt.

Now, as she sat across from him in the busy bar, she wondered what possessed her to agree. She felt like a fish out of water. Nick, on the other hand, looked right at home and seemed to know everyone. He made introductions and small talk with those that stopped by their table. Some lingered around longer than others, but generally, they all moved on.

"So, is this where you normally hang out?" she asked, looking around. The place was busy and catered to a sophisticated crowd. She was glad she opted for a casual red wrap-around dress, strappy heels and minimal makeup. She didn't stick out as much as she would have in her yoga pants and tank top.

"I sure do," Nick said as he leaned back in his chair and studied the two women at a nearby table.

"Oh, don't let me cramp your style," she said, noticing where his gaze wandered. Men, they were all the same.

"Jealous?" he said, focusing all of his attention on her.

"Don't flatter yourself," she scoffed. "You're not my type."

Nick leaned forward, folded his hands on the table and looked at her studiously.

"What exactly is your type then?"

Ava sloshed her wine in the glass. She wasn't going to play his games.

"My type," she said. "Is none of your business. Just know that you're not it."

"Awww," he said mockingly. "Now you've hurt my feelings."

"As if."

Nick watched her across the table and wondered why he asked her to come. He didn't mind the gig and was actually surprised at how much he enjoyed it. It was interesting to see the case progress, just as it was frustrating when it hit roadblocks. Ava wasn't the worst person he'd ever worked with, but she made it clear he was a means to an end.

She had a great face, he thought. Maybe he could talk her into doing a photo session. When she wasn't so prickly and oblivious to the world around her. Come to think of it, she wasn't really his type either. He preferred his women to be less bossy.

His thoughts were interrupted by a couple that suddenly appeared at their table. He had a friendly smile, straightforward manner and bore a remarkable resemblance to Nick. She was shorter, with a mass of blonde curls and undisguised curiosity in her blue eyes.

"You must be Ava," she said, extending her hand. "I'm Odessa, and this is Steve."

"I'm Nick's cousin," Steve explained as he shook her hand.

Ava welcomed the unexpected company with curiosity. After short introductions, Odessa and Steve jumped into entertaining stories about Nick, who took their teasing in stride. They kept the conversation light and breezy. Ava was glad she decided to come out after all. Occasionally she caught Nick looking at her and rolling his eyes.

"So, Ava," Odessa said. "Nick tells us you're a podcaster."

"I am," she confirmed. "I have a true crime podcast called The Missing Voices. It focuses on finding missing people."

"Why would you hire this guy?" Steve said as he nudged his cousin with his elbow. "Surely you could have found someone better."

"You'd be surprised," Ava told him. "Besides, Nick is actually a good assistant."

"Oh, come now, boss," Nick laughed. "I can't take all this praise. It's too much. True, but too much."

They all laughed. Ava shook her head in mock disbelief. Maybe he wasn't as horrible as she thought he was. She enjoyed Odessa and Steve's company as well, thinking of how nice it was to have someone so close to you that you can always depend on.

"Investigating cases must be so exciting," Odessa said with admiration. "Do you ever feel, I don't know, afraid?"

"Afraid?"

"Old cases, missing people. Poking in the past must make some people nervous. Aren't you scared that someone might not like what you find?"

Ava contemplated the question. Occasionally she got odd messages but no threats. At least no so far. But before she had a chance to elaborate, Odessa suddenly stopped and stared at something behind them.

"Don't look now," she said, grabbing Nick's arm across the table. "Nicole is here."

There was a sudden change in the air. Ava felt like she was the only one who had no idea what was happening. She didn't have to wait long for Nicole to make herself present.

Ava watched with amazement as she made her way to their table. She was dressed to kill in a tight black dress and five-inch heels. Her hair was long, her makeup flawless, and there was fury in her dark eyes. She was razor-focused on Nick, and it was clear she already had a few drinks in her.

"So that's how it is," she snarled at him while slamming her hands on the table. "This is what you call working things out?"

"Nicole," Nick said quietly, his eyes flat. "We've talked about this already."

"Talked about it? You said you needed some time, and instead, you're hanging out with this basic bitch?" She eyed Ava with disgust. "Like what the fuck?"

Before anyone could do anything, Nicole grabbed one of the glasses on the table, her nails flashing like sharp claws, and threw its contents in Nick's face. "You're gonna be sorry, asshole."

Ava watched the exchange in fascination as Nicole turned to her. The commotion at their table had everyone staring. The music stopped, and as if on cue, two security guys appeared behind Nicole. They grabbed her just as two other women tried to talk her down. They dragged her out, kicking and screaming.

Nick took the napkins Steve offered him and wiped his face. Their waitress brought more napkins and helped mop up the mess. Not knowing what else to do, Ava laughed.

"I'm sorry," she said, waving her hand. "I thought my exes were bad."

That seemed to cut the tension. The music resumed, and people went on about their business.

"In that case, let's get another round of drinks here," Steve said with relief. "I feel like we're going to need them."

"I knew I like you, Ava," Odessa said as she leaned over. "I think you and I will get along just fine."

***

Several hours later, Nick and Ava stumbled home. Grateful that the bar wasn't far from home, they took their time cutting through the neighbouring streets. The night was still warm, but you could feel the summer coming to an end.

Nick shoved his hands in his pockets and walked beside her. This was the first time he saw Ava not focused on work or irritated with him. She was always so intense and consumed by finding justice. Her eyes were always so sad.

Tonight he learned that she loved to dance and sang in the shower. That was essentially thanks to Odessa, who befriended her like he never could. Some part of him wanted to find out more about her. Another part told him to let it go. Their arrangement was temporary and strictly professional.

"I'm really sorry about tonight," he said.

"You mean Nicole?" she laughed. "Your taste in women is none of my business."

"It's not that," he said, "Nicole has a habit of showing up and making a scene. Seeing me with you probably triggered her."

"Oh please," Ava rolled her eyes, then stopped. "Hold on. I think I have a rock in my sandal."

She stopped and looked around. Finding a bench, she walked over and sat down. Nick watched as she fumbled with her shoes. Since he didn't want her to think he was staring at her, he sat beside her on the bench.

"Nicole and I broke up a while ago," he offered. "That's why I moved back home."

"You really don't have to explain things to me. Many people move in with their parents. What's the big deal?"

"It's a bit more complicated than that," he rubbed his jaw. "We were engaged."

Ava looked at him with curiosity. "I see."

"I couldn't go through with it," he said, staring into the distance.

"Why not?"

"I don't know."

"Did you tell her that?"

"I told her I needed more time," Nick sighed.

That was six months ago. He told Nicole he needed some time to work things out and then moved out. She was furious and demanded he come to his senses. That was definitely not going to end to her liking. Nick was sure there was no future for him with Nicole.

"That makes more sense now," Ava said. "I'm definitely not an expert on relationships, but it seems like you need to figure things out with her. But, your personal life is none of my business."

She rose from the bench and started walking again. Nick got up and followed her.

"Tell me how you really feel," he teased. "And here I thought we were becoming friends."

"Did you now?"

They laughed some more as they walked down the walkway that led to their respective homes. They stopped awkwardly at the bottom of the stairs that led to the porch.

"Well, thanks for coming out," Nick said.

"Thanks for inviting me out," she said. "I had a nice time."

"So did I."

They stood there in the moonlight. Something about the night, or maybe it was the alcohol, made him lean towards her.

"Ah, what are you doing?" she asked, poking him in the chest.

"What?"

"What?"

"Were you trying to kiss me?" he asked, his voice a little slurry.

"In your dreams," she laughed. "Good night, Nick."

She left him standing there as she strolled inside.

CHAPTER 8

The next day, Ava, Nick and Stan faced the garage filled with junk and layers of dust. Stan, his hands planted firmly on his hips, looked like an aging archeologist ready to discover buried treasure.

"I think we should look at this the same way we look at an archeological dig," he told them. "Don't roll your eyes at me, Ava. It's very unbecoming."

"Grandpa, this is a garage filled with junk. It's not an archeological site," she said.

Stan looked at her with a smile.

"Ah, but there are many similarities," he told her. "What do you think we find at most archeological sites? Old trash. That's what. Broken pottery, everyday objects and tools. Don't even get me started on the animal bones and human excrement."

Ava groaned while Nick chuckled. This was going to be more fun than he expected.

"I got the bins set up as you asked," Nick gestured to said bins lined up beside the garage. "Trash, keep and donate. Pretty standard."

"Excellent," Stan pulled up the bandana hanging on his neck over his mouth and nose. He was like an excited child ready to hit the playground. "Let's do this."

After removing a few of the oversized items in the front, they divided the garage into sections, each of them tackling a different one. Ava sorted through gardening tools in various shapes, broken pots and rusty tins. There were ropes, hoses and empty jars. So far, most of the things she found were trash. It was surprising how much of it accumulated over the years.

As she dug through her section, not expecting to find anything useful. She was tired, slightly hungover and not in the mood to deal with Nicky's chirpy attitude. He tackled the opposite side of the garage, happily chatting with Stan about every item they came across. This was definitely a waste of time.

"Would you look at this," Stan said as he pulled an old red and yellow tricycle from under some broken chairs and raised it like a prize to show Ava. "Your tricycle. I remember when you used to ride it up and down the street pretending you were driving a racing car."

"Really now," Nick said with a smile. "And yet you still don't have a license."

"Shut it," she said without looking at him. "I clearly had no idea about the wonders of public transit, and this convenient thing called a car service."

"I remember it, just like it was yesterday," Stan said, ignoring them both. "You had all these ribbons tied to the handles because you thought they would help you fly."

"If I was racing a car, why would I need ribbons to fly?" she said and gave Nick a look when he laughed.

"That's the beauty of a child's imagination," he patted her on the shoulder. "There are no limits."

Stan took the tricycle outside and set it by one of the bins. He wiped the back of his hand across his forehead and assessed their progress. Even a few hours in, they barely made a dent. There was still so much to go through.

Nick came out and dumped more junk into the trash bin. He was sweaty and full of dust. There were so many other things he could be doing, yet here he was, helping out his cranky boss. He walked over to where Stan stood, staring inside the garage. He was the real reason Nick came over to help.

"You should take a break, Stan. You look a bit flushed," Nick said. "Ava and I can do some more digging. Besides, we're not going to go through all of this in one day."

"You're right, Nick," he said after a moment. He didn't want to pass on the opportunity to find more treasure, but he was exhausted. "I'm gonna go inside and rest for a bit."

Nick reached for his water bottle and drank. There was so much dust in the garage, he could feel it all stick in his nose and throat. He couldn't wait to grab a shower and wash off the layer of dirt and grime he was currently covered with.

Inside, Ava tugged at another box, trying to loosen it as she nudged it closer. She found a small plastic flower pot and used it as a step stool. It gave her enough height to get a better grip on the box. She pulled again, just as Nick walked back inside the garage.

Before he had a chance to say anything, the box suddenly shifted. Ava lost her balance as the flower pot cracked under her weight and sent her staggering backwards. He managed to catch her just as the box fell on them.

"You okay?" he asked as dust went flying everywhere.

"Yeah," she said between coughs. "What the hell was in that box?"

The box tore open when it hit the floor. Ava reached inside to see what was in there. Inside were several tools and a metal case, similar in size to a toolbox. It was slightly beaten up, but overall it was in good shape.

"What do you think this is?" she asked.

"One way to find out," he said. "Open it."

"It's locked."

"Let me see," Nick took the box from her. "We can probably pick the lock."

"Or," she suggested. "We can go inside and see if my grandfather has a key."

Nick didn't argue, seeing this as a sign that they were done with rummaging for the day. They locked the garage and went inside to get Stan.

"I've never seen this box before," he said thoughtfully, rubbing his chin. "It's definitely not mine. Should we crack it open?"

They all stood around the table, eyeing the mystery box before them. After trying out different tools, they finally managed to pry it open with a screwdriver.

"Holy shit," Ava whispered as she lifted the lid. "This is Sharon's stash."

***

The box, once neatly organized, was in disarray. There was an envelope filled with film negatives, several floppy disks, a notebook, a couple of 35mm film rolls, and a small camera.

"It's like a time capsule," Ava said in awe as she picked through the items. "Hey, Nick, do you know how to get these developed?"

Nick picked up the old camera like it was a timeless classic. Then again, he never met a camera that didn't fascinate him. He wondered if he could talk Ava into letting him have the camera.

"When I first got into photography," he said. "I was totally into experimenting with 35mm cameras. I spent days on end taking pictures and playing in the darkroom. I know a place where I can get these developed, and I know a way to see what's on those film strips."

"Do you think we can get anything off them?" Stan asked. "After so many years, they are probably ruined."

Nick held up several strips of the negatives against the light, then put them back in the envelope.

"Negatives can easily last for a couple hundred years and even up to a thousand in proper conditions," he said. "However, "proper conditions" is the key here. The heat can destroy them very quickly, and since they were stored in the garage with no central air for so many years, it's hard to tell what conditions they are in."

"What about the film?"

"Same goes. The images are still here on the negatives, so that's a good sign," he lifted another strip against the light to demonstrate. "But, it's difficult to say how much of the original has faded over the years. I won't know about the quality of what's on the rolls until we actually try to develop the film."

Ava tapped her fingers impatiently on the table.

"How long is that going to take?" she asked. "And what about the disks? We need to know what's on there. Sharon wouldn't have kept them unless there was something important there."

"Ava," her grandfather said calmly. "We don't even know what we found. But I can help with the floppy disks."

"You can?" they both asked, surprised.

"Of course," Stan said as he took the disk from her. "What do you think people used to save their documents on? These little disks. I got one of those floppy disk readers to access some of my original work. I still have it somewhere around here, or maybe it's at the office. Then we can print whatever is on them."

Although Stan was retired, he still occasionally gave lectures and talks at the university. Because of that, he had his own desk in a shared office space on campus that he used from time to time.

"You're full of surprises, Grandpa."

Stan smiled sheepishly, then shrugged it off.

"I think we can safely say that today was a rewarding day. Even if the two of you did most of the work," he said. "Why don't I order some food, and we call it a day."

They regrouped when the food arrived. It was something that has become a habit as of late, Ava thought. The three of them, grabbing dinner together. That definitely wasn't part of his job description.

Ava wondered if that was why Stan liked having Nick around. She hasn't been visiting her grandfather as much as she should have. He never made her feel like she was abandoning him, but truth be told, she was. Her father had Joan, but her grandfather only had her since her grandmother died.

Maybe she could make Toronto a more of a permanent home, she thought as she chowed down on pizza. A base where she could live and work and keep Stan company.

***

The following day Ava started the day off with a run. It was a lovely, crisp morning with some of the summer vibe still in the air. Today's playlist reflected her mood – it was fast, upbeat and loud.

Finding Sharon's box was a small victory. Just when she thought things weren't going anywhere, the information literally fell in her lap. Now, she needed to figure out what was on the disks and film. She firmly believed, just like she told Stan and Nick, that Sharon wouldn't hide things if they weren't important.

Ava made her way towards the Danforth, jogged in place at the light, then continued south towards Withrow Park. At this time of day, the park was mostly filled with joggers and dog walkers. She ran down the path that crossed it, making her way west through the streets towards Riverdale Park. The massive park, sloping west of Broadview Avenue, had, in her opinion, one of the best views of Toronto.

She stopped for a moment to admire the view when she heard someone call out her name. It was Kevin, waving at her across the street. He walked over to her side, a coffee cup in his hand.

"Hey, Kevin," she smiled. "How nice to see you."

"You know me," he said, blushing slightly. "Once a coffee addict, always a coffee addict. How are you?"

"I'm great," she beamed. "Just out for a run."

"You sure seem to be in a great mood," he observed.

"You could say that," she said.

"Oh, do tell," he asked, intrigued. "Is there a special someone in your life?"

"What? No."

"Well, in that case, why don't we sit on the bench here, and you can fill me in," he suggested. "If it's not a new man, then what?"

They walked over to the bench that overlooked the city and sat down.

"It's nothing concrete," she said after a moment. "But I have a feeling that we might be closer to figuring out why Sharon was killed."

"That's great," he said. "The cops find anything new?"

"Not exactly," Ava shook her head.

Kevin studied her as if trying to read her mind. A broad smile lit across his face.

"It's you," he said excitedly. "You found something."

"Maybe I did, or maybe I didn't," she said noncommittally.

"How exciting," he grinned. "Do you want to include an update on your mom's case at the meetup? I'm sure everyone would love to hear it."

She thought about it for a moment, decided against it.

"I don't want to take attention away from the case we're featuring," Ava said. The meetup was several days away, and she wouldn't have anything concrete by then anyway.

"Of course," Kevin nodded with understanding. "But you have to definitely do an event about Sharon's case once you have it all figured out."

"You got it," she smiled. "I gotta head back."

As she got up from the bench, a red Jeep stopped by the side of the road. The driver honked and waved at Ava.

"You know him?" Kevin asked, nodding at the driver.

"Unfortunately, I do," she said. "That's my assistant, Nick."

"That guy is your assistant?"

"Yeah," she nodded and left Kevin staring as she walked towards the Jeep and got inside.

"Who's your boyfriend?" Nick asked. "Look how sad he looks."

"He's not my boyfriend," Ava said as she fastened her seatbelt. "Did you get the stuff?"

"I did," he said as he merged back with traffic. "Were you out for a run?"

"What are you, a cop?"

"Just making friendly conversation," he said. "What got into you? Did you get in a fight with your sad-looking boyfriend?"

"Shut up."

***

"Where do you want the scanner?" Nick asked as he looked around the office.

"I'll make some space on the desk," she said as she moved things around. "That way, I can copy everything directly to my files."

Nick set up the flatbed scanner on Ava's desk. It was slightly larger than a standard laptop. Since hers didn't have the required software, they had to hook it up to Nick's. That meant more shuffling of papers and screens.

"Do you really need this many screens on here," he asked as he looked for a way to connect the scanner to one of the monitors and an external hard drive.

"Are you sure you can get it to work?" she asked.

"What would I do without all this praise? "Nick said mockingly. "You should know better by now. Whoa, wait."

Ava's hand stopped in mid-air. "What?"

"You don't want to get your fingerprints on it," Nick said and took the envelope from her hand and set it back on the table. He reached inside his bag and pulled out a new set of latex gloves, then carefully put them on and got to work.

Ava observed him clean the strips with an air blower before loading them on the film trays. He slowly snapped the lid closed and made adjustments in the software before initiating the scan. The machine hummed quietly as the image slowly appeared on the screen.

"They don't look like much," she said, leaning over his shoulder for a better look. "Are you sure this is the best way to do it?"

"There are several ways to scan negatives," Nick said, trying to ignore the way her hair brushed against his arm. He shifted slightly, forcing her to straighten, putting some distance between them. "This was the quickest way, but if there is anything here that you want to develop or preserve, it will take longer."

"What do you mean?" she asked.

"We are using a scanner like this one because it scans multiple strips at once," he said. "You can easily use a DSLR or a mirrorless camera with a micro lens. You put the negative on a light table or a light box to illuminate it and then photograph each frame. The rest is the same."

"That sounds complicated," she noted.

"Once you set everything up, it's not that complicated. It just takes time."

"So this is the faster method?" she asked dubiously. "Even this looks like it will take forever."

"Scanning them is only part of the process," he said. "You still have to adjust the images on screen after they are scanned. Otherwise, you're still looking at negatives."

"Great," Ava said and checked her watch. "I'll leave you to it. I told my grandfather I'd go with him to look for the floppy disk reader."

"Take your time," Nick told her. "This will take a while."

While Nick continued working on the negatives, Stan and Ava went to his office at the university and got the reader. They decided it was better to print everything at home in case they found any sensitive information.

"What is this?" Nick asked as he flipped through the pages Ava printed.

"It looks like accounting ledgers or banking statements, maybe," she said as he filled his plate with more lemon potatoes. "No idea who they belong to."

"Was that all that was on there?"

"Pretty much," Ava told him. "I checked all the disks, but since they were all full of these accounts, I only printed some of them. It's enough to get us started."

"Are you going to let Tyler know what you found? I'm sure he'd love to hear from you."

"Stop being such a child," Ava said as she rolled her eyes. "I left him a message. At this point, we still don't know for sure that this has anything to do with why Sharon ended up dead."

"She wouldn't have these records if they weren't important."

Ava didn't answer right away. The accounts proved that Sharon was up to something. Still, she couldn't figure out if the records would exonerate Sharon or prove that she was blackmailing someone. At this point, Ava herself wasn't sure if she was ready for the truth.

CHAPTER 9

The process of scanning the negatives took longer than she anticipated. They worked late into the evening and finally had enough images to work with. There were several of Ava as a baby, but the rest were all Sharon. Group shots with classmates, friends and several with Michael. They both looked happy.

Ava examined the images of her parents. She knew they met in university, so she wasn't surprised to see them with people she assumed were their classmates. Candid shots of faces she didn't know or recognize. Graduation shots of Sharon in her gown and cap holding flowers. Her father standing with her, proudly smiling at the camera.

They were so young, almost the same age as her, but with so much more experience. The pictures showed snapshots of a time Ava was very unfamiliar with. A life of two people who made her, only one of them raised her. Both were unaware of what the future had in stock for them when those pictures were taken.

"I don't see anything here that gives us anything new," she said, disappointed. "I don't know what I expected, but I really hoped there was more."

Nick watched her frown at the screen. He could feel her disappointment, but he could do nothing to change what was on the negatives. Her feelings weren't his concern. The job was.

"Have you seen any of these pictures before?" he asked as he crossed his arms.

"No, I don't think I have."

"They might not give you the answers you were looking for," he told her, "but there must have been a reason why Sharon kept them."

She considered his words. Individually these images were random, but altogether there was a common thread. Different places, people and events, but they meant something to Sharon.

"Happy times," Ava said as she leaned against the desk. "These are all reminders of what made her happy."

"Yes, they definitely are," Nick said as he looked at the images on his screen. There was Sharon, beaming at Ava with her hair in little pigtails. Sharon with Ava in the park, playing with dolls, laughing. These were definitely happy memories, and they meant something to Sharon.

"Do you think the rest of the film is going to be the same?" she asked. "You know, more shots of happy times?"

"Hard to tell, but we'll find out tomorrow," he said and checked the time. "Now, I have to get ready for my date."

"Don't let me keep you then," she said absently as he left.

She looked through the photos again. Trying to understand her parents as they were in those pictures. Her grandparents had other albums of family photos stashed away. Were these ones there too?

Curious, she went downstairs to look for the albums. It didn't take long to find what she needed. Growing up, Ava used to flip through the pages hoping to feel closer to her mother. Eventually, they stopped being comforting and stood as a reminder of what she lost. It's been a while since she looked at them.

Memories flooded back, many a sad reminder of the past. Maybe this wasn't a good idea after all. Ava snapped the album shut. A loose picture fell on the floor. She picked it up.

It was a group shot taken at what looked like a house party. Her parents were among the cheerful party-goers, but so was another familiar face that shouldn't have been there. She took another look. This didn't make sense. Had her father lied to her?

***

Traffic in the city was a killer. With construction still in full swing, many city roads were cut down to one lane in each direction. Nick tried to avoid the main roads, but he didn't fare better on the highway. Here too, the cars moved at a snail's pace through the elevated stretch of the artery weaving through Toronto's downtown core.

Usually, Nick enjoyed the drive through the condo-littered downtown with the top down on his Jeep and the breeze blowing through his hair. But not today. He was exhausted. His date with Amber the night before was a bust. Based on her profile, she should've been a perfect girl for him.

Smart, attractive and not looking for a commitment. She flirted outrageously with him all night, teasing at what awaited if he went home with her. But he didn't. Like a sucker, he made excuses about having to work in the morning and spent the night tossing and turning instead. That would teach him a lesson.

The morning's photoshoot was out of the city, so he had to leave early to get there on time. That gave him time to think and kick himself again for declining Amber's tempting offer. The job took longer than he expected, and now he was stuck in traffic. That means he didn't have time to drop off the film at his buddy's place to get developed. That would have to wait till tomorrow.

Nick could already hear Ava in his head. He could already picture her disappointment when he told her about the film. She wouldn't say it, but her disapproval would be clear.

Ava was relentless, even stubborn at times, and expected everyone else to work like her. There were times when she irritated the crap out of him. She didn't think much of him, that was clear, but he never gave her a reason to complain about his work.

There was darkness wrapped around her like a shadow, and occasionally, he caught glimpses of darkness inside her. She chased ghosts, digging for answers even when there were none. That was her deal. He had no interest in dealing with that.

Today, she would have to take that prickly personality and shove it. He wasn't in the mood to deal with her. Maybe he could avoid her for the rest of the day and reach out to Amber instead. He could probably talk her into continuing where they left off the night before.

With traffic at a standstill, Nick decided to take the next exit and try his luck on the road. He maneuvered the car to the left lane and joined the line of cars trying to get off the highway. He glanced at his navigation system, trying to figure out the fastest route. At this rate, he was better off taking Lakeshore all the way east than heading north on one of the streets that would take him home.

There was probably enough time to drop by The Acropolis and grab some food. He could text Amber from there while he waited. As the plan formulated in his head, his mood improved significantly. He turned the radio up and tapped his hand on the steering wheel to the music as he waited for the light to change.

He almost missed it. A slight movement in his rearview mirror caught his attention. There was a car, a dark sedan with tinted windows, that he was sure was there when he left the photoshoot. Granted, he wasn't the only one driving back into the city, but there weren't many other cars taking the exact same route home.

On a hunch, at the next set of lights, Nick made a right, leading him into the small industrial area away from the residential neighbourhood he initially planned on taking. The dark sedan switched lanes as well and got in the turning lane several cars behind him.

He was at a certain disadvantage. It was harder to hide his bright red Jeep than it was to blend in with a dark sedan. Whoever was following him was careful enough to stay on his tail for this long, which concerned him. Nick cursed under his breath. If he wasn't so distracted, he might have noticed the car earlier.

To ensure he didn't imagine things, Nick made a few more random turns and switches. The dark sedan remained discreetly in the distance. There was no way to get a clear view of the driver. Debating his options, Nick pulled into the parking lot of a large shopping plaza. Whoever was following him would have to park if they wanted to follow him out of the car.

Nick slowly navigated the parking lot without spotting the sedan. He either managed to lose them, or they lost interest. He might have imagined the whole thing, but the more he tried to convince himself of that, the less likely it seemed. The question was, who wanted to follow him and why?

There was only one person with a grudge against him that came to mind – Nicole. But sneaking around wasn't her style. He dismissed the idea. He thought briefly of his slashed tire. Was this the same person?

Nick decided to head home. If the sedan was still following him, he would deal with that then. But as he made his way out of the plaza, he didn't spot any suspicious cars. No dark sedans followed him home.

As he waited for his food, Nick messaged Amber to make plans. Reluctantly, he left a message for Ava about his weird experience with the dark sedan.

***

Ava woke up tired after a restless night. She wasn't looking forward to the conversation with her father. It was bad enough that her mother could have been a blackmailer. It was another to find out that your father cheated on her.

She looked at the picture again. There it was, the face that shouldn't have been there—her stepmother's. What was Joan doing at a party with her parents? They weren't supposed to know each other then.

In the picture, Sharon sat on the couch, smiling at the camera. On her left was a man with a laughing woman on his lap. On her right was Michael, his hand on Sharon's leg, his head twisted slightly so that he looked at the woman behind Sharon, Joan. His other hand reached out for Joan as she leaned towards him.

According to her father, he didn't meet Joan until after Sharon's disappearance. Clearly, that was a lie. She had seen her father and Joan look like that at each other many times. Like there was nobody else in the world but them. This picture implied that they knew each other, possibly intimately, even then. Did Sharon know what was going on?

Ava needed answers. She called her father, but this time went straight to the point.

"Explain this," she said when his face came on the screen. She shoved the picture to the camera and watched his face turn pale. "Why is Joan in this picture?"

"It was a party," he said, but there was a hitch in his voice.

"You told me you met Joan after Sharon disappeared," she said accusingly. "This proves you lied."

"Ava, it was a party," he tried to keep his voice steady. "There were many people there."

"Dad, I'm not stupid. I've seen you and Joan look at each other this way before," she brought the picture closer to the camera. "This is not a picture of two people at a random party who forgot they knew each other."

Michael looked down and closed his eyes. He sighed.

"Joan and I had a relationship before I met Sharon," he said slowly. "We loved each other deeply."

"What happened?"

"She was married," he said, looking ashamed. "Look, I'm not proud of it. Neither one of us planned for it to happen. But it did."

"Why not get divorced?"

"It was a different time, Ava," he told her. "I worked for her husband. He was a tenured professor. An affair would have ruined us all."

So her father and Joan had an affair? She had a hard time picturing her strait-laced father having an affair with his boss's wife.

"Did Sharon know?"

"I don't think so," Michael raked his hand through his hair. "It was complicated. Joan thought her husband was getting suspicious, so we called it off."

"But Sharon found out about it."

"Yes," his eyes went flat. "Sharon found out the truth after it was over."

Ava always suspected her parents' relationship wasn't perfect. Still, childishly she believed that they would have gotten back together if Sharon stayed. But the more she investigated it, the more it looked like there was very little love between them.

"How did you end up with Sharon?"

"I was her teaching assistant," he said, resigned. "She was this brilliant, fascinating woman. I was heartbroken after Joan, and I split. Sharon was there, and she made it clear she was interested in me. She was intoxicating. Smart and beautiful. I was, naturally, taken by her."

The truth wasn't easy, but he had lived with guilt for so many years. Finally, saying it out loud was freeing.

"Ava, I'm sorry I never told you the truth," he said. "Sharon and I were never meant to be together. It was a mistake. We were two very different people who didn't love each other the way we deserved. When Joan's husband died, we rekindled our relationship. Sharon found out, and she was furious. She demanded a divorce, and I agreed. I gave her whatever she wanted so I could be with Joan."

So the truth was uglier than she thought. "Did Grandpa know?"

"I don't think so," he said. "I gave Sharon whatever she wanted in exchange for not telling anyone about the affair. One of those conditions was that I never deny your grandparents time with you. I kept that promise. I don't think they ever knew the truth."

"Are you going to tell him?"

"There is no point in telling him the truth after all these years. It won't change anything. There are no bad feelings between us, and I'd prefer to keep it that way."

Ava shut off her laptop. The call certainly didn't go as she expected. She tried to put herself in Sharon's shoes. How would she feel if she found out her husband was having an affair with an old flame? Would she be furious? Vengeful? Betrayed?

She tried to see things from her father's side. Did he hate Sharon that much? What did it say about her, the daughter he had with the woman he never loved in the first place.

***

She needed to get out of the house. Ava hit the street and kept running. The world felt like it was closing in on her, and she couldn't get out. The ground under her feet was shifting with every step while she tried to keep up.

Why didn't they tell her the truth? Ava recalled what her father said about Sharon. I was glad she was out of my life. She didn't doubt that for a second. With Sharon gone, nothing was standing between him and Joan. Well, except for her, but that was quickly taken care of.

It was all too much to take all at once.

Usually, running helped her think. Today, it felt as if her mind was running faster than her feet. She ran down the street, stopping briefly at stop signs, checking for oncoming traffic out of habit.

Ava didn't know what to think. She was exhausted, but at the same time, there was too much energy pent up inside her. The more she dug into Sharon, the more she didn't like what she found.

Her grandfather didn't believe his daughter was capable of theft. She didn't share the theory about blackmail with him, so she wouldn't upset him. He would never believe that Sharon was capable of such actions. But, what if she was?

Ava stepped on the street when someone yanked her back. She narrowly escaped getting hit by a car.

"You okay?" the man said, as she nodded.

They both watched the car disappear down the street.

"You should be careful," he told her. "Crazy drivers out there, I tell you."

"Thanks," she said. "I'll be careful."

Still a bit shaken, she decided to head back home. Her heart was still pounding somewhere in her ears as she tried to get her bearings. That man saved her life. Here she was angry at the world, meanwhile, it all could have ended in a flash.

That was one way to put things in perspective. Once she figured out what happened to Sharon, she would focus on her life. Maybe date some more. She should ask Nick what he used to find dates. She just wasn't as versed in dating apps as he was.

Speaking of Nick, she thought. Where was he?

Ava realized she left her phone at the house. She knew he had one of his pre-existing gigs today, but she hoped he had a chance to get those photos developed. She was really curious to see what Sharon had there.

Even if Sharon turned out to be a blackmailer, Ava thought, that would give them a sense of closure. She clearly had lots of things going on in her life at the time, including becoming a single mother. Was she as clever as everyone said she was, or was she an innocent woman set up to take a fall?

She would need to check in with Detective Burnett again to see if he made any progress. Maybe he would be able to shed some light on the accounts they found on the disks.

Ava almost reached for her phone again, just to remember that she didn't have it. She picked up her pace, eager to get home and make some calls. Maybe she could talk Nick into dinner so she could bounce some ideas off him. He was definitely less annoying when he ate and listened. Then again, she paid him to listen to her.

By the time she got back, the anger had subsided. Ava couldn't wait to get back to work. Maybe she'd even call her father and apologize for being an ass. What happened between her parents and Joan was between them, not her.

She found Nick sitting on the steps in front of his house. He was texting impatiently on the phone. Since he wore a dress shirt with his jeans instead of his regular t-shirt, she assumed he was going out on a date. Looks like she was going to work alone.

She called out to him as a car roared by. It had one of those ear-splitting mufflers that made the ground vibrate underneath her feet. Nick looked up from his phone and noticed her waving.

Suddenly, a deafening sound ripped through the otherwise quiet neighbourhood. Her ears were ringing, and she tasted blood and dirt. She realized she was lying face-first on the walkway, and the blood was hers. She was disoriented, but someone was shaking her, saying her name. Then everything went dark.

CHAPTER 10

Nick got an urgent call from a client as he was about to leave for his date with Amber. A quick conversation resolved the issue, but now the client wanted some additional quotes. He sat down on the porch steps and typed out a quick email with the requested information. It was better to send it now and not have to worry about it later.

He heard Ava call out his name as he looked up from his phone. Whatever she planned to say next was cut off by a piercing roar of a car. It was loud and obnoxious. He winced as he hit send then got up to talk to her.

What happened next became a blur. One minute Ava was walking towards him, then next, she was down. The blast sent debris all over the lawn and the sidewalk, but all he could see was her body on the ground. Time slowed, and panic ripped through him like a thunderbolt. He ran to her, screaming her name. She was dazed, her eyes unfocused as he held her in his arms. Then she went limp.

Sirens wailed in the distance. Car alarms blared on the street, and people shouted around him. Nick was oblivious to it all. Every second felt like an hour rolling by him in slow motion. He has never had anyone die in his arms before, and he didn't want to start now.

"Shit, Ava," he muttered. "Stay with me. Stay with me. Help is coming."

Someone grabbed his shoulder and shook it. It was Stan, his face filled with fear. He kneeled beside him, calling Ava's name and stroking her head. When her eyes finally opened and blinked, both men felt a sense of relief wash through them.

"You're okay, baby," Stan told her, smiling through tears. "Just hang in there."

Ava squeezed his hand then looked up at Nick. His eyes were wide, and his face was several shades paler.

"What happened?" she asked, trying to sit up. She looked around them with confusion.

"It looks like an explosion," Nick gestured towards the remnants of the garbage bins on the curb. "The paramedics are here."

Nick stepped aside, letting the EMTs do their job. The place was crawling with cops, firemen and nosy onlookers. The damage seemed minimal, contained to the bins on the curb by their house. It was hard to say whose bins were the target, but it was clear they either belonged to Stan or his parents.

Nick gave his statement to the police, keeping an eye on Ava, who was treated by the paramedics.

"Any idea who might want to hurt you or your girlfriend?" Officer Tan asked him while he scribbled in his notebook. He seemed to be the one in charge.

"Oh, no. She's not my girlfriend," Nick said. "We're neighbours. I work for her. It doesn't matter. Do you think this was intentional?"

"Hard to say at this point," Tan said as he surveyed the damage. "It looks like a homemade dry ice bomb. Teenagers often use them as pranks. More stupid than devious but dangerous just the same. If we're lucky, we'll get fingerprints and maybe get a match in the system. Meanwhile, here is my card in case you can think of anything else. We'll be in touch."

Nick took his card and walked over to the ambulance where Ava was still being treated. She had a small cut on her temple and some scrapes on her knees and hands. One of those space blankets was wrapped tightly around her. She looked up when she saw him approach.

"Thank you," she said.

He shrugged and winked at her. "Just doing my job, boss."

"Other duties as assigned?" she teased. Her smile died suddenly when she spotted a fresh bloodstain on his shirt.

Nick saw her pale as she stared at his chest. He looked down and noticed the stain.

"That's my blood," she said almost in a whisper.

"It's nothing," he said assuringly. "People bleed on me all the time."

A ghost of a smile touched her lips. "You're dressed up," she said as if she just remembered. "You were going out. Now you have blood all over your shirt."

Nick looked down at his shirt again, his date with Amber, now a distant memory.

"Nah," he said. "I have nowhere to be. But I think these nice paramedics are going to take you in for a checkup."

Nick watched them load her up in the ambulance.

"I'll see you at the hospital," he called out before the medics shut the door.

***

Ava sat cross-legged on the sofa, holding a mug of tea while Nick filled her in on the dark sedan that followed him home. She was sporting a bandaid over the cut on her forehead, her hair pulled back in a loose ponytail. She was still sore from the fall, so they relocated their workspace to the living room for the time being. Loose-fitting pants draped over her scraped knees, now covered up with bandages. She tried not to wince.

"Do you think whoever followed you was the same person that slashed your tire?" she asked.

"I don't know for sure," Nick said as he leaned back in the big armchair. "If we assume that whoever slashed the tire drove that dark pickup truck, then they either changed cars, or there are more people involved."

"And you're absolutely sure you were followed?"

"I guess it could have been a coincidence," he shrugged. If it was any other day, he probably wouldn't have thought twice about that. "But that's way too much of one not to be connected."

"Do you think the explosion yesterday was connected?" she asked.

"Yes," he said without hesitation. "I think someone is sending us warnings."

Ava sipped the tea as she considered his words. She also wasn't a huge believer in coincidences. The information they uncovered so far didn't provide any huge revelations about Sharon's death, but maybe the killer, or killers, didn't know that.

"Someone doesn't want us going around asking questions," she thought out loud.

"Could it be her killer?" Nick asked.

"It's possible," she agreed, then added, "there was something else that happened yesterday that might be connected."

She told Nick about almost getting hit by a car and the good samaritan that moved her out of the way. A seemingly random incident that could be dismissed as an accident. Unless you looked at it as another piece of the puzzle.

"I didn't really think much of it," she continued. "I was too caught up in my own thoughts."

"Did you see what the car looked like?"

"No," she shook her head in frustration. "It could have been a dark sedan, but it also could have been something else. My mind is blank."

Nick considered an idea in his head. "Could the good samaritan have been a plant? You know, make it look like he saved your life while he knew all along what was going to happen?"

"I don't think so," she dismissed the idea. "I've seen him around. He lives in this neighbourhood."

"Well, there goes that idea."

The mystery around Sharon Novak's disappearance seemed to deepen with each passing day. Ava felt like they were getting closer to getting answers, but they were still mainly in the dark about what happened.

"Did you get the film developed?" she asked. "I totally forgot about it."

"No, I didn't get a chance yesterday," he said. "I can go and drop it off now. Want to come along?"

Ava winced as she stretched out her legs. Her head still hurt a bit, and her vision got fuzzy if she stared at her computer screen for too long.

"Might as well," she said. "It's not like I can get a lot of work done today anyway. Have you seen my phone?"

She looked around the room, forgetting where she left it.

"I forgot it when I went out yesterday," she explained. "I don't know where it is."

They searched the house and found Ava's phone in her office. It was completely dead.

"Bring it with you," Nick told her. "I have a cable in the car. You can charge it there."

They drove across town to drop off the film. Ava watched the cars zip by, keeping an eye out for a dark sedan. She tried not to think about the fact that someone out there was potentially watching her right now.

When her phone beeped, she picked it up. The battery had enough juice to hold for a bit as she checked her messages. She looked over at Nick while she listened to his message. His voice was steady as he recounted the incident, telling her his suspicions. The following two messages were from Kevin and Lori, confirming the details for the meetup.

"Everything okay?" he asked.

"Yeah, just getting messages from yesterday," she said as the next one played in her ear. "It's Frank Mitchell."

"What does he want?" he asked.

"I'm not sure," Ava said as she saved the message. "He said he has something to tell me about Sharon. It sounds urgent. He said to come when I can."

Nick pulled the car over to the shoulder and stopped.

"I take it we're going right now?"

"I think we should," Ava said. "Meanwhile, I'll try to call him."

***

Ava tried calling Mitchell several times as they drove, but there was no answer.

"Maybe he went out," Nick suggested. "Or maybe he can't hear the phone. Or the battery is dead."

"Yes, it could be any of those things," she sighed. "Why couldn't he just tell me in the message what he needed to say?"

"Some people are better at talking face to face," he pointed out. "We're almost there, so you'll find out soon enough."

The house was quiet as they drove up. There were no black pickup trucks in the driveway or anywhere near the house. It was eerily quiet as they knocked on the door.

But it wasn't Mitchell who answered. The woman was petite with a crop of short, spiky hair, pale complexion and puffy eyes.

"Yes?" she said absently. "Can I help you with something?"

"You must be Mrs. Mitchell," Ava said. "My name is Ava Reed, and I was hoping to speak with your husband. Is he here?"

"Frank?" she said as her eyes filled with tears. "You're here to see Frank?"

"Yes," Ava tried again. "I spoke with him a few days ago. Yesterday he left me a message asking me to come to see him."

"You haven't heard, then," she said, clutching her hand to her chest. "Frank's in a hospital."

Ava and Nick exchanged a quick look.

"I'm sorry to hear that, Mrs. Mitchell," she said. "What happened?"

She gestured for them to come in and follow her inside. Just like the last time, the house was quiet, with the occasional sound of a motorboat gliding across the lake. Unlike the last time, the house was in disarray. She seemed oblivious to everything around her.

"Can I get you anything?" she asked as if she suddenly realized there were guests in the house. "Some water, maybe?"

She then plopped on the couch between two piles of clothes like a deflated balloon.

"That's okay, Mrs. Mitchell," Ava said, taking a seat across from her in one of the chairs not yet covered with belongings. "Can you tell us what happened?"

Nick stood at the side as Mrs. Mitchell looked away towards the window, her eyes filled with grief.

"I went to the store just for a few minutes," she said. "I wasn't even gone that long. When I came home, I found Frank at the bottom of the stairs."

Her tears were dangerously close to spilling out like a flood. "They said it was a heart attack. He's in the hospital. Unconscious."

"I'm sorry to hear that, Mrs. Mitchell," Ava said.

"Thank you," a vague smile crossed her lips. She looked around the room absently as if looking for someone.

"Frank left me a message yesterday to come and see him," Ava tried again. "Did he mention anything to you? About me or maybe a woman named Sharon Novak?"

"No, Frank didn't talk about his work," she said. "He must have called you when I was out."

"So you don't know what he wanted to tell me?"

"I don't, I'm sorry," she sat with her hands folded in her lap. "Frank has high blood pressure. That's why we moved here after he retired. For peace and quiet."

She dabbed the corner of her eye with a tissue. "Frank isn't in the best shape, but he is trying to be healthier. And now he might die anyway."

Ava thought about the beers Frank was pounding back the last time they were here but said nothing. It was perfectly plausible for a man like Frank Mitchell to have a heart attack. But that seemed very coincidental.

"Mrs. Mitchell," Nick asked. "Was Frank worried about anything lately? Anything or anyone bothering him?"

"He was a bit agitated lately," she said. "But that's Frank. He's always complaining about something. He doesn't tell me anything."

"That's okay," Ava got up and handed her a card. "If you remember anything, give me a call. I hope Frank has a speedy recovery, Mrs. Mitchell."

***

"Another coincidence?" Nick asked as they got back in his Jeep.

"Definitely a convenient one," Ava said.

"Well, I didn't see a black pickup truck anywhere."

"I don't think that was him in the truck," Ava said. "When we left him, he wasn't in any shape to drive."

"So either someone was watching the house, or he called someone."

Nick drove slowly down the driveway and stopped at the end of it.

"The truck must have come from somewhere," he said. "The town we stopped at was south of here. I think we should do a little cruise around the area and see if we can find it."

They drove around for a couple of hours but couldn't find a black pickup truck that matched the one they saw tear out of the parking lot. There were several similar-looking vehicles, but none were what they were looking for. It started to get dark when they decided to abandon their search.

"I would suggest stopping in town for a bite," Ava said. "But after what happened the last time, I am not sure that's a good idea."

"Well, we could drive by the restaurant and see if the truck is there," he suggested. "Of course, we could be wrong, and it was someone else entirely."

The truck wasn't parked at the restaurant, but they noticed another road that led to the parking lot. Since neither one remembered seeing the truck drive into the parking lot past them, nor saw it parked in the lot when they got there, they assumed it came from there.

"Should we see where this road leads?" Ava asked.

"We've come this far, "Nick shrugged. "Might as well. But then we really have to stop for food. I'm starving."

"Deal."

The road led them away from the centre of town through an industrial area with several large parking lots and warehouses. At this time of day, there wasn't a lot of activity going on. They drove for several minutes past the industrial area as the road split into a fork.

"Where to?" Nick asked.

"Well," Ava said as she glanced at her phone. "Left goes back to town. Right will take us back to the highway back to the city."

"How far is the highway?"

"About a fifteen-minute drive," Ava told him. "We could go back to town to get food, or we can just wait till we get back to Toronto. It's less than an hour's drive back."

Reluctantly, Nick made a right and headed down the dark road.

"We should really stock up on some snacks," he said. "If we're going to go on these long-ass drives."

They drove in silence for a while. Nick's was the only car on the road with the occasional one passing by in the opposite direction. They didn't notice a dark pickup truck parked behind a tree as they passed by.

"I totally forgot to ask how your date went," Ava said to break up the silence.

"My date?" he said. "What about it?"

"How did it go?" she asked again. "Unless, of course, it's none of my business."

Nick thought of Amber and the missed opportunities. There was no way she would give him another chance, but that wasn't something he was going to tell Ava.

"It was fine," he said dismissively. "Nothing to write home about."

"Oh," Ava hesitated. "Ah, I was going to ask what dating apps you use."

"Why?" he said. "So you can find me and see if we match?"

"Why in hell would I want to do that?"

Nick only laughed, but after a few moments, his laughter died as he looked in his rearview mirror.

Suddenly a black pickup truck drove up behind them. As Nick watched it speed up, the driver turned on the lamps mounted to the roof rack. The blinding lights made it impossible to see who was driving or see the road in front.

"Fuck," Nick swore as he tried to maneuver the Jeep away from the other vehicle. "Hang on tight."

Ava grabbed onto anything she could as the seatbelt dug into her flesh. As Nick sped up, so did the car behind them. The pattern repeated several times until the truck hit the back of Nick's Jeep, pushing it forward. He sped up to get away, just as the truck rammed into the back of the Jeep again.

"Who the hell is that?" Ava managed. "I can't see anything with these damned lights."

Nick slammed on the gas and floored it. It took them several minutes to realize that the truck fell behind and wasn't following them anymore. Once they were a fair distance away, the driver cut the lights, disappearing under the cloak of darkness.

"Let's get the hell out of here," Nick said as they finally got on the highway.

CHAPTER 11

Detective Burnett sat across from Ava and Nick in his office as they recounted their visit to Mitchell's home and the truck that tried to run them off the road. On his desk was a metal box Ava found in her grandfather's garage.

"It would probably be best that you two don't venture out anywhere near Mitchell's place," Tyler told them. "I'll try to do a run on the vehicle, but without the plates, I can't guarantee that we'll find anything."

"Can't you get anything off Nick's Jeep?" Ava asked.

"We can definitely give it a go," Tyler turned to Nick, "can you leave your vehicle in our shop for a couple of days? If we're lucky, we'll get some transfer paint from the truck that hit you. It would help to narrow down the search."

"Yeah, I can do that," Nick said. "The damage isn't as bad as it could have been, considering."

"It seems that you're making someone nervous," Tyler noted. "I checked with the lead investigator on the dry ice bomb, and so far, there are no prints."

"So you think the bomb and the other incidents are related?" Ava asked.

"At this stage, we can't eliminate any possibilities. If you like, I can assign some officers to keep an eye on you."

"I think it's fine," Nick interjected. "As long as we stay in the area. Most of these incidents happened out of town."

"You can never be too careful."

"I think Nick's right," Ava said. "We just need to stay close to home. Have you had a chance to check in on Mitchell's condition?"

"I made some calls," he said. "There is no change in his status. Nothing about his condition indicates any foul play."

"It just seems too much of a coincidence."

"Stranger things have happened," Tyler said as he shrugged. "You want to tell me about this box? You said it belonged to your mother."

"Yes," Ava said. "Inside, we found some negatives, floppy disks, rolls of film and a notebook."

"We haven't been able to get the film developed yet," Nick told him. "With everything that's happened in the last few days."

"You've been busy," Tyler said as he opened the box and picked up the printed pages. "Is this what's on the disks?"

"Yes," Ava nodded. "They look like financial statements and accounts, but I have no idea who they belong to."

Tyler put down the paper and picked up the notebook. He flipped through the pages as Ava and Nick sat in silence.

"I know what you're thinking," Ava said as Tyler's eyes met hers.

"Like I said, there are two possibilities as to why Sharon was murdered," he said. "She either found something that she wasn't supposed to and was killed for it. Or, she took what she found and tried to bargain with it."

"You mean blackmail," Nick said flatly.

"We have to consider all possibilities. Even if the answers are not what we hoped for."

Ava didn't say anything, but she knew how this looked. The documents would either exonerate Sharon or prove she wasn't as honest as her grandfather believed. There was a reason she kept track of accounts and bank statements, but she was the only one who knew why.

"Could these documents clear her?" she asked.

"I'd have to take this all in and have our forensic team look at it in detail," Tyler told her. "You can leave the rolls of film with me or get them developed yourself. If there is anything useful on them, let me know." When she hesitated, he added. "I promise you that none of this will go missing. It's safe to leave it here."

"I know," Ava said as they got up to leave. "I made copies of everything anyway. We'll take the film, though. Are you still coming to the meetup this afternoon?"

"Yes, it's in my calendar."

After they left, Tyler laid out all the items on his desk. He took out the small key found with Sharon's remains out of the evidence bag. It didn't fit the box Ava found. He was still unable to figure out what it opened.

Since the key didn't belong to Sharon, it was likely her killer left it behind. Most likely dropped it when they dumped her body. Since forensics didn't find any blood or shell casings on the scene, it looked like she was killed elsewhere.

What did you find, Sharon? Tyler wondered as he logged onto his computer and got to work.

***

Ava met Lori for lunch at The Acropolis. Right now, it was probably one of the safest places in the city, and the food was excellent. Plus, she didn't think anyone would try to hurt her here.

"I can't believe someone set off a dry-ice bomb by your house," Lori said. "Have they found out who did it?"

"Not yet," Ava said. They covered the meetup scheduled for later that evening and the logistics that went with it during lunch. As much as she wanted to put what happened behind her, there was no denying that someone wasn't happy about her investigation into Sharons' death. Lori listened in disbelief as Ava filled her in on the event of the past few days.

"I'm glad you're okay," Lori said. "You are okay, right?"

"Oh, yeah, I'm fine," Ava said dismissively. "Just a little bit bruised from the fall still. Nick's car got some damage from last night, but it's not as bad as it could have been."

"Ava, you have to be careful," Lori said. "You don't know who you're dealing with."

"I wish I did," she admitted. "It would be so much easier. Right now, nothing about this makes sense. Why would anyone want to harm me?"

"It looks like they are trying to scare you off," Lori said. "But people like that always mean business. If they had something to do with Sharon's death, they probably wouldn't hesitate to hurt you too."

"If they did have something to do with Sharon's death," Ava said. "That's more of a reason to keep going to find out the truth."

"I don't know about this, Ava. I feel better knowing that you have that assistant working for you," Lori said. "Where is he, by the way? I was looking forward to meeting him."

Ava picked up her phone and checked it for messages.

"He went to get the film developed," she said. "If he's not back in time, you'll meet him at the event."

"Are you going to hire him permanently, or should I keep looking for suitable candidates?"

Ava didn't answer right away. She got used to working with Nick, but their arrangement was temporary.

"Oh, he has his own thing going on," she said. "I doubt this is something he would even consider. Especially after what happened last night. Besides, I'm going to start working on the new season of The Missing Voices soon."

"You know, you don't have to move every time you work on a new season," Lori told her. "You choose to go to where the cases take you and stay there before moving on to the next one."

"It's how I work best," Ava said. "You know that. I like developing a connection with the families and being where it all happened."

"You know what I think?"

"I'm sure you're going to tell me anyway."

"I think that you leave because you're running away," Lori said. "You've been chasing Sharon's ghost for so long you forgot how to live."

"That's not true."

"Isn't it? You're great at what you do because you relate to people whose cases you investigate," she said. "You care about the families. You feel their pain and what they are going through. And by channelling all of yourself into every case, you're reliving Sharon's case over and over."

"You're wrong," Ava said defiantly.

"Am I, though?" Lori said gently. "I'm just telling you how I see it."

"Are you my shrink now?"

"I'm your friend. One that worries about you," she said.

Before she had a chance to respond, Odessa rushed over to their table with a big smile on her face.

"I hope I'm not interrupting," she said as she sat down at their table. "I'm just grabbing some takeout. I'll be out of your hair shortly."

"Oh, don't worry," Ava said as she introduced the two women. She wasn't surprised when the two became immediate friends.

"I have an idea," Odessa said as she got up to pick up her food order, "Since you're here another day, why don't you two come out tomorrow night? We can have a girl's night."

"I like the sound of that," Lori agreed. "Ava?"

"Sure, "Ava laughed. "Text me the details, and we'll do it up."

***

Nick met Ava and Lori at the event, getting there minutes before it started. She noticed Tyler in the audience as well. Ava almost missed him dressed casually in jeans and a t-shirt. He

also sported a ball cap. If she didn't know him, Ava would
have never pegged him as a cop.

This wasn't the first time she's done one of these events,
but that didn't mean she enjoyed them. Ave watched people
mingle, recognizing some of the faces from previous events.
While she wasn't a member of any murder mystery club, she
had attended as a guest speaker. New ones were popping up on
every corner, inviting her to speak.

Crime and murder tended to bring out the worst in some
people. The morbid curiosity often disguised as a willingness
to help pissed her off. Those people showed up at these events
not to help but to get a fix for their true crime addiction.

 Ava wasn't naïve. She started her own podcast to
capitalize on the collective fascination with the suffering of
others. But she didn't do it for entertainment value. It gave her
purpose. While most people switched off the show after
getting that fix and moved on with their lives, there were
countless families of the victims who couldn't. She knew what
that was like. She was one of them. Ava didn't need to live
vicariously through the stories. Her life was very much like the
stories she covered.

She couldn't overlook the entertainment value the podcast
held for others, so she made it her mission to focus her show
on the people behind the stories. Ava meticulously researched
the cases, interviewed the families and law enforcement if they
were willing. Sometimes these episodes led to solid leads that

helped close some of the cases. That alone made events like this one worthwhile.

As the event's organizer, Kevin took his role seriously. The monthly meetups brought many true crime fans together to talk about both unsolved and solved murder cases. Attendees often discussed their own theories of famous and lesser-known cases. Occasionally, they watched true crime documentaries together and discussed them afterwards. It took all kinds, she supposed.

After the standard opening greeting and introductions, Kevin opened the floor for Ava. She gave an overview of the recent seasons of the podcast, the cases and fielded questions like a pro. Those that didn't know her would have assumed she loved every minute of it, but Nick could see the strain and struggle within. She hid it well.

"You know why her podcast is such a hit?" Lori asked Nick as he sat beside her in the audience. "She is every story she tells. They are all very personal to her, no matter the case."

"She hates this," he looked around at the crowd. "She hates being here. Why does she do it then?"

"It's what drives her," Lori tilted her head slightly to look at him. He had an intensity about him that, as a flesh and blood woman, she could appreciate. No wonder Ava kept him all to herself. "She's been chasing Sharon and others like her, most of her life. Running is what she does best. The podcast, events like this, they are a means to an end."

Nick considered her words as another hand went up. A short brunette with a round face stood up by the mic.

"Are you gonna do a season or a series about our mother's case?" she asked Ava. "You know, like a more detailed look at what happened to her?"

Ava expected someone to ask the question when she agreed to do the event. There was no getting around it. She caught Burnett's eye, but his face was blank.

"As many of you might have heard, my mother has been found, and she's no longer missing," she told the audience. "At this time, her murder hasn't been solved, and the investigation is still ongoing. I have previously done an episode on her case on my show, and you might have heard me talk about the case on other podcasts."

She looked over at Lori, who gave her a slight nod.

"I started my podcast to give families an avenue for sharing the stories of their loved ones, just as I have done for my mother. Having said that, I've been in talks with my producer about the possibility of creating a season of The Missing Voices dedicated to the story of Sharon Novak or creating a separate show about it."

There was a brief murmur of voices as more hands shot up in the air. A tall thin man with a short crop of blond hair and matching goatee stood up.

"Is there a suspect?" he asked.

"Do the police know who did it?" asked another voice at the same time.

"What happened to the three million dollars?" someone else demanded.

Questions fired from the audience like lightbulbs from paparazzi cameras. Ava tried not to let them get to her. She could feel her heart beating in her throat, and her hands felt clammy. The audience was slowly turning into a mob.

"Everyone, stop talking" Kevin stood up, his voice rising over the audience. "I know everyone is excited about this case, but let's keep things civil. Ava is here as our guest, and this is not an interrogation." He glanced over at her, giving her a reassuring smile. "Is there anything else you'd like to add?"

"Only that the investigation is still ongoing," Ava said, trying to maintain her calm. "When I can share Sharon's story, I'd like it to be a complete one. To do that, the police must do their work first, and I'm working closely with them to find out who did this to her."

Ava sat through the rest of what was left of the event and bolted the moment it was over.

***

Tyler had mixed feelings about amateur sleuths. The majority of them were people who considered themselves crime solvers after watching crime shows and binging on true crime podcasts. In reality, they were driven by fantasies built around solving crimes rather than actual experience or knowledge. They preferred over-the-top conspiracy theories and elaborate possibilities while often dismissing the tedious, which often led to actually solving cases.

But the fact was many amateur detectives, in addition to their craving for true crime, had means that police often didn't. Many murder cases went cold due to a lack of resources. People, unfortunately, don't wait for the old cases to be solved to inflict pain on each other, and there is only so much manpower to go around.

Tyler remembered the toll old cases took on his grandfather. They stayed with him long after he had retired. He would have loved the crime community's quest for answers and their inventiveness. Tyler was used to getting wild theories and useless tips from armchair sleuths. Every now and then, there was a crumb or a seemingly random memory that helped him solve a case. Those were rare, but they made a difference.

None of the cases mentioned in Ava's podcast had anything to do with him. Still, Tyler found himself drawn to them anyway. He could definitely admire all the work that went into each episode and often wondered about the investigations professionally. Ava was a great storyteller and had a way of humanizing the victims.

Yes, Tyler smiled. Grandpa would have liked Ava. The fact that she cared so much would have meant a lot to him.

Tyler's mind snapped to attention the moment the first question about Sharon came up. The conversation escalated quickly, and he could see Ava tense up in front of the crowd. He looked around, searching for anyone that looked out of place, which was challenging in a group of true crime-obsessed fans.

There was no uniform look that could set someone apart from the group that was already so versatile. From teenagers to the middle-aged. Men and women of different backgrounds and walks of life, linked by their obsession with true crime.

Tyler considered intervening but opted to let it play out. Ave held her own and didn't disclose any vital information about the investigation. She looked a bit frazzled by the questioning but didn't give up. He knew that getting amateurs involved in police work had its risks, even if they were family members of the victim. He hoped he wasn't wrong by getting her involved. Then again, if he didn't, she was doing quite well on her own.

As Tyler mused about overly enthusiastic crowds, his phone vibrated. He didn't recognize the number, and before he had a chance to answer, it went to voicemail. As the crowd mingled, he left to look for a quiet spot and called his voicemail.

There were two messages. He deleted the first one and skipped to the second. As he listened, he felt a chill go down his spine. Frank Mitchell was dead.

"Shit," he murmured as he went back inside. The meetup was still in full swing as the crowd buzzed with excitement. Since Ava was still busy, he decided to send her a message later as he made his way out.

CHAPTER 12

After the adventures of the last few days, Ava welcomed the distraction a night out offered. She sighed as Lori handed out shot glasses filled with alcohol. She closed her eyes, tossed back the clear liquid and let the alcohol coat her throat.

At this point, they were all tipsy, fuelled by the dance music pumping through the speakers. Ava looked over as Odessa laughed at something Lori said, but she continued to sway to the music. She was still sore, but the alcohol helped to dull the pain.

And to think that she woke up that morning seriously tempted to get out of the girls' night deal. But Lori wouldn't take no for an answer, and Ava found herself in her hotel room as they got ready for their big night out. Even Nick encouraged her to go out. She suspected that he wanted her busy elsewhere so he could go out himself.

Now, several hours of dancing and copious amounts of alcohol later, Ava decided a night out was exactly what she needed. For all she knew, Nick was out on a hot date, which was none of her business.

"You know what?" she told her companions with a drunken grin. "I'm glad we did this. All of it."

"Girl, that's why I've been trying to get you to come out for ages," Lori laughed. She turned to Odessa and pointed at Ava. "She never wants to come out. It's like pulling teeth with her. Every single time."

"Then you should come to Toronto more often, and we can do this again," Odessa said, moving some of the empty glasses away from their drinks. "You now have two friends in town."

Her companions hooted like drunken sailors sharing a joke. She rolled her eyes, then downed the remains of her drink and set the empty glass on the bar. Ava lost count of how many drinks and shots they consumed. She was pretty sure they drank their weight in booze. It was edging close to the last call at the bar when they decided to call it a night.

They stumbled artfully outside. It was a warm evening, and the streets were filled with party-goers in various stages of inebriation. Ava felt great. The light breeze felt so good against her skin. But now, she was exhausted and wanted nothing but her bed. Ava took out her phone to request a ride when she heard Odessa's voice.

"Ahhh, look," Odessa beamed. "The guys are here."

Ava looked in the direction she pointed. Steve and Nick were leaning against the Jeep, watching them. Odessa stumbled into Steve's arms as she giggled.

"We drank a lot," she told him.

"Yeah, I can tell, baby," he laughed, stroking her hair. "Let's get you home."

They said their goodbyes. As Steve guided Odessa into his car, Lori gave Ava a quick hug. Her ride pulled up smoothly at the curb seconds later, and she slipped artfully inside.

Nick leaned against his car, arms crossed as he watched Ava hesitate. After a brief pause, she walked up beside him and leaned against the car. His hot date must have ended already, she thought.

"Fancy running into you here," she said.

"Thought you could use a ride, boss," he said as he brushed the bangs out of her eyes. "And, I brought food."

"Chicken souvlaki?" she asked hopefully.

"With extra tomatoes," he winked at her. "Just how you like it."

"Sold."

Ava didn't realize how hungry she was until she stuffed her face with food. With all the alcohol she consumed over the last several hours, this was precisely what she needed. She glanced over at Nick as he navigated the streets. Dressed in jeans and a t-shirt, with a ball cap sitting backwards on his head, he had that no-care in the world look that suited him so well.

Sensing her staring at him, Nick looked over and smiled.

"What?" she asked.

"You starting to get sweet on me?" he teased.

"Don't flatter yourself."

"Nothing to be ashamed of, you know."

"You wish."

Nick smiled as he drove. Ava didn't even realize she was dozing off until the car stopped. Nick opened her door and helped her get out.

"How much did you drink?" he asked as she practically fell into his arms.

"Too much or not enough," she said. "Depends on who you ask."

"There is that," Nick held on to her, guiding them along the walkway. "Watch your step."

The moment they stepped on the porch, Nick sensed something was off. Stan's door was slightly ajar. The light he typically left on when Ava was out was also dark.

"Wait here," he said, instinctively trying to hold her back.

"What?" she asked. "What's wrong?"

He pointed at the open door. "Let me check it out first."

But she was faster. Not giving Nick a chance to stop her, Ava pushed past him and ran inside. The house was dark, illuminated only by the glow coming from the streetlight outside. She darted upstairs and stopped short at the top of the stairs.

"Oh my god, Nick," he saw her kneel beside Stan, her voice frantic. As he followed her up the stairs, he could see a body lying on the floor.

"I think he fell. Grandpa?" she called out, reaching to check his pulse, tears already streaming down her face.

Nick flipped on the hallway light, and it became clear that Stan didn't just fall. Someone bashed the back of his head with something heavy. There was blood pooling around him, and there was a trail of debris all over the floor. A quick glance down the hallway told him that someone had ransacked Ava's office as well. It looked like Stan most likely interrupted an intruder.

He kneeled down beside her, took out his phone and dialled 911.

***

She felt numb. The hours blended together like a horrific nightmare. Ava barely remembered the paramedics arriving at the house, taking her grandfather away. The cops questioned where she was, where Nick was, trying to establish a timeline. All she could think of was Stan lying on the ground, bleeding all over the floor. It was like a bad dream she desperately wanted to wake up from.

Nick sat down beside her and handed her a cup of coffee. She took it, staring absently into space. It didn't take long for the coffee cup to heat up. She felt the warmth even though her hands felt like blocks of ice. She looked down at it as if surprised to see it there, then took a careful sip and set it down again. It tasted like nothing.

"He's still in surgery," Ava told him, her eyes puffy and red from crying.

"He'll be okay," he said. "It takes time."

"I should have stayed home," she said. "I should've been home instead of getting drunk at the club."

Nick let her lean against him and put his arm around her. "You can't think that, Ava. It's not your fault."

"It sure feels like it."

"World is full of what-ifs, and you can't blame yourself. Look," he told her. "If you were home, you could have been hurt too. You could be the one lying in surgery right now."

"You don't know that."

"Neither do you," he pointed out. "Whoever did this would have found a way in whether you were there or not."

Ava closed her eyes and absently rubbed her face. She knew he was right, but the guilt was still there. She reached for the coffee cup, took another sip then set it down again. She was so cold even with the sweatshirt Nick gave her to put over her skimpy top.

"How much do you want to bet that this is related to Sharon's case?" she asked, rubbing her hands together. "The bomb, the dark sedan, the pickup truck. It all started after we found her box."

"You think this is another message to warn you off?" he asked.

"They were looking for something," she said. "We're making them nervous."

"We have to assume that they think we have what she hid," he pointed out. "Whatever it is they think we have must be the key to what happened."

"They must have thought we hid it inside," she said. "They don't know that we gave it to Burnett."

"Maybe they think Mitchell gave us something, and they want it back."

"Yeah, that could be it too," she said thoughtfully.

"You did make copies of everything, right?"

"Of course. I digitized everything and uploaded it to the cloud," Ava said, feeling some of the control coming back. "I also have a backup USB stick hidden in the house."

"We also have the pictures from the film," Nick pointed out. "They're at my house."

The sliding door interrupted what she was going to say next. They both looked up, expecting a doctor with an update on Stan's condition. Instead, Odessa rushed inside with Steve at her heels. They were both dressed in sweats and looked like they just got out of bed. Odessa went straight to Ava and wrapped her in a big hug.

"Oh, Ava, I'm so sorry about your grandfather," she said. "We came as soon as we heard. Nick texted to tell us."

"Thank you," Ava said as she hugged her back and realized that she meant it. "Thank you for coming."

Odessa pulled back and looked at her closely. "Did you get any sleep? You must be exhausted."

"Not really," Ava admitted. She knew she was starting to crash, but the worry kept her up. "I couldn't sleep."

"We came here straight from the house," Nick told them. "They took our statements, and we did a quick walk through the house. Then they roped it off with police tape."

"I know," Steve said. "We drove by on our way here. Have you had any news yet?"

As if on cue, the door slid open again. They all stood up, waiting for news. A woman in green scrubs holding a clipboard came out to greet them.

"I'm Dr. Hansley," she said, scanning their faces. "Are you Stan Novak's family?"

"He's my grandfather," Ava told her as she stepped forward.

The doctor checked something on the clipboard, "You must be Ava."

"I am. How is he?"

"Your grandfather sustained traumatic brain injuries," Dr. Hansley explained. "There is significant swelling, and it's putting pressure on his brain. The pressure reduces blood flow and oxygen supply. We had to put him in a medically-induced coma to help decrease the swelling and to protect the brain from further damage."

"Is he going to be okay?" Ava asked. "A coma sounds bad."

"Not necessarily," the doctor assured her. "A medically-induced coma gives the brain time to rest and heal."

"Can I see him?" Ava asked.

"He's not responsive right now," Dr. Hansley said. "But I can let you see him for a few minutes. I'm sorry," she looked at the rest of them. "Family only at this time."

Ava followed her to where Stan lay in bed, hooked up to monitors and breathing tubes. He seemed so pale and frail. It was one thing to go after her, but to hurt an old man who never did anyone any harm was another. She would find who did this and see them punished. That was something she could do for him.

***

Tyler reached out to the locals regarding Frank Mitchell's death. A heart attack in a man his age combined with heavy drinking and many health issues wasn't unusual. Without concrete evidence, there wasn't much they could do. An autopsy was unlikely since the death wasn't considered suspicious unless the family requested one.

There wasn't much evidence left on Nick's car, making it challenging to identify the truck that tried to run them off the road. There were no cameras at the parking lot behind the restaurant, so that was another dead end.

Tyler was tired and cranky when he logged on to his computer. He checked for updates on the items from Sharon's box. The answer was always the same. The forensic team was dealing with many cases, and his evidence was in line. He hated the seemingly endless layers of bureaucracy.

Tyler scrolled through emails when an alert caught his eye. There was a break-in at Stan Novak's house. Interesting. He read over the report and felt alarm bells going off in his head like fireworks.

"Shit," he muttered to himself. After the recent incidents, he set up an alert on the system to notify him if anything popped on the address or related to Ava, Stan or Nick's names. Now it did. He checked the time and decided to head over there.

On the way, he tried calling Ava, but the call went straight to voicemail. The house was still taped off, so he tried Nick next door. He answered almost immediately. His hair was sticking out in all directions, and the sleepy look in his eyes told Tyler he likely woke him up.

"Detective Burnett," Nick said as he scratched his chin. "Come in."

Tyler followed him inside. Taking one look at the pillow and blanket on the couch as they passed the living room into the kitchen. The Laskaris house was almost a mirror image of Stan's with a few more recent updates. Judging by the décor and the family photos, this was very much Nick's parents' house. Tyler wondered how they felt about their adult son moving in and messing with their routine. Then again, they have been away for some time, so maybe that wasn't an issue for them.

"Would you like some coffee?" Nick asked him as he turned on the coffee maker, stifling a yawn. "Ava is still sleeping upstairs."

"Sure, black is fine," Tyler said and sat down at the kitchen table as Nick pulled out two mugs and set them on the counter. "I heard what happened next door. Any updates?"

"Stan's in a medically-induced coma," he said, then rubbed his eye and yawned. "Ava is devastated. She thinks, well we both do, that this tied in with the other incidents."

"It does look connected," Tyler said. "We're working on the documents from the floppy disks, trying to find anything useful. Can you tell me what happened last night?"

"Ava went out, some ladies' night deal. I was out with my cousin Steve," he explained. "His girlfriend Odessa was out with Ava. We went there to pick them up. They went home, and I brought Ava back here. We noticed that the door wasn't locked, and the porch light was off. Stan always leaves the light on outside when Ava's out."

"What did you do next?"

"We walked in, and then she ran up the stairs before I could stop her. Anyway," Nick shook his head. "She found Stan upstairs. There was blood on the floor, and the upstairs was a mess. I called 911."

"Did you notice damage anywhere else in the house or just the office?

"Mostly in the office," he said and got up, grabbed the coffee carafe and poured the hot liquid into the mugs. "We did a quick walk-through with the officers, then went to the hospital."

Nick drank his coffee as Tyler scribbled something in his notebook.

"Did you notice anyone following you or Ava after the last incident?" Tyler asked. "Anyone suspicious hanging around? Paying more attention than usual?"

"No, I don't think so. We've both been a bit paranoid lately, but we haven't noticed anything unusual."

"You can tell her that the house should be released shortly," Tyler told him. "By the way, did you get the pictures developed?"

"Sure did," Nick smiled for the first time. "I'll grab them for you. I don't know how much they will tell you, though."

Tyler flipped through the photos, and Nick's words became clear. The pictures were of accounts and ledgers. He'd bet his ass that those were copies of the ones from the floppy disks.

***

Ava woke up feeling like she'd been hit by a truck. Slowly, she opened her eyes and looked around the strange room. Everything from the night before came back in a flash, like a nightmare she couldn't wake up from. The only minor difference was that she wasn't dreaming, and this was real life.

She was in Nick's bed, wearing what looked like his shirt. She barely recalled getting back here and arguing with Nick about where she was going to sleep. She was relieved to wake up alone. Not that anything would have happened, but still.

Feeling a little self-conscious, she looked around the room for her belongings. She needed a shower and a change of clothes. On the floor, she spotted her overnight bag. Feeling relieved, she grabbed it and looked inside. Her toiletries, extra clothes, and make-up were all there. She would have to thank whoever picked it up from Lori's hotel room and brought it over.

She found a clean towel on the nightstand with a note from Nick letting her know it was for her to use. She grabbed the towel and her bag and ventured out of the room. Then made a beeline for the bathroom and winced when she saw herself in the mirror. Her hair was a mess, her make-up smeared all over her face, and her eyes were puffy and red. Fittingly, she looked as bad as she felt.

Nothing, a hot shower, fresh clothes, and a hairbrush couldn't fix. Twenty minutes later, Ava made her way down the stairs. She found Nick watching TV on the couch in a hoodie and sweatpants.

Nick looked up and smiled when she walked into the room. Her face was flushed, her wet hair pulled back in a ponytail. Remembering how pale she looked at the hospital, Nick was glad to see some colour back on her face. She hooked her thumbs on the belt loops of her jeans and smiled.

"Hi," she said, then pointed at the pillows and blanket. "Did you sleep on the couch?"

"Yes," he told her. "Maybe it's stupid, but I thought that whoever broke in could try here next."

"So, you slept here because you thought this was a better position to fight off a potential intruder?" she asked.

"Well, yeah," he said like it was obvious. "We've had cars following us, trying to force us off the road. Someone slashed my tires. Set a bomb to scare you."

"Okay, okay, I get it," Ava made her way to the oversized loveseat across from him. "Thank you for everything you did last night. I couldn't have done it without you."

"You're welcome."

"I bet you didn't expect so much action when you signed up to be my assistant," she smiled.

"I think I need a raise," he said with a mocking frown. "Or at least some type of hazard pay. By the way, Detective Burnett stopped by."

"Did you give him the pictures?"

"Yes. He said you should be able to get back to the house soon."

"Great, thank you," she looked around for her phone. "I have to make some calls."

Nick went to make coffee to give her some space. She checked in with the hospital, listened to her messages, and updated Lori and Odessa. She checked her emails and finally called her parents.

The call was surprisingly brief, and he could hear the frustration in her voice as she tried to explain what happened. Judging from the one-sided conversation he could listen to, she wasn't very good at convincing them that everything was under control.

He walked over and handed her the cup with coffee. It was strong and sweet, just the way she liked it. Nick watched her close her eyes as she inhaled the steam before she took a sip.

"My god, this is exactly what I needed," she said. "I hate to repeat myself but thank you. Again."

"You're welcome," he sat down on the couch. "How did it go with your parents?"

"It depends on how you look at it," she sighed. "They are insisting on flying down."

"And that upsets you?"

Ava opted to drink more coffee before she answered. She wasn't ready to face her father and Joan about their relationship.

"Let's just say that I recently found out that my father hasn't been the most forthcoming with certain information," she said. "I'm not ready to deal with that right now."

"Wanna talk about it?"

"I'd rather not."

"Your call," he got up, took her hand and pulled her up. "Let's get some food in you, and then we'll go to the hospital to check on Stan."

"You really don't have to do that," she told him but followed him to the kitchen anyway. The rumbling in her stomach told her not to be a fool and eat something.

"Yeah, yeah," he waved his hand dismissively. "Now, let's see what's here to eat."

CHAPTER 13

They stopped by the hospital. There was no change in Stan's condition. Disappointed, they went back to Nick's and worked there over dinner.

"It feels like we haven't made any real headway," Ava said as she looked over her notes. Fortunately, she had her laptop with her when she went over to Lori's hotel room, so it wasn't damaged during the break-in.

"Someone seems to think that you have," Nick pointed out as he grabbed another slice of pizza. "The question is, what do they think you have?"

It would appear that even twenty-five years later, Sharon's killer didn't want the world to know what she found. The fact that someone broke in and rummaged through Ava's office told her that it was still a threat to them.

"I don't think they know what I have," she said thoughtfully. "They didn't know exactly what they were looking for, so they trashed everything. Think about it. Wouldn't it make more sense to break in, grab what you were looking for and leave without leaving any evidence of being there? Leaving a mess and attacking an old man is definitely going to raise flags."

"Maybe that was the plan," Nick suggested. "Then Stan came upon the intruder, and they panicked. Hit him over the head and took off."

"Very plausible," she agreed. "But, did they trash the office then attack Stan, or was it the other way around?"

"Does it matter?"

She thought about it for a moment. "In a way, yes. Trashing the office first means that someone is going to hear it. Why make so much mess and noise?"

"Because you're frustrated that you can't find what you came for," Nick said as he followed her train of thought.

"Exactly. Even if they attacked Stan first, they could have made it look like an accident. No mess in the office, no evidence of a break-in," she thought out loud. "They could have pushed him down the stairs, and nobody would have thought much about it. An old man fell down the stairs. A tragic accident."

"That's cold," Nick said as he looked at her with curiosity. "Should I be worried about what you'd do to me if I piss you off?"

"Haha," she rolled her eyes. "Aren't you a funny guy?"

"Hey, I'm just trying to figure out what I've got myself into," he told her as he wiped his hands and logged onto his own laptop. "Let's go back to Sharon. Tell me about her. Not as your mother, but as the case."

"All right," she agreed and opened her files. "Sharon got a degree in business, which she followed up with an MBA, with a specialty in finance. She liked numbers and, by all accounts, was a wiz with computers. She knew the financial ins and outs and how to manipulate numbers. The original investigation leaned heavily on this. The police used that as to why she stole the money."

"But they never proved that she stole any money, nor did they find it," Nick continued. "Of course, maybe they had a reason not to look that hard into the case."

"Frank Mitchell knew something he wasn't telling us. For a seasoned investigator, he did a piss poor job of the investigation. I've seen more detailed reporting from rookie cops," she said thoughtfully. "He interviewed Sharon's coworkers, who had surprisingly little to say about her. The story was pretty much the same for everyone – she was intelligent, ambitious, friendly and outgoing. Nobody noticed anything and had no idea what could have happened to her."

"Convenient," Nick said. "But that's not how it works. People who work together often socialize with each other. We did when I worked in an office. That hasn't changed over the years. There must have been someone in that office with whom she went out for drinks or had coffee. She must have talked to someone about what she found."

Ava checked her notes. Including Sharon and her boss, there were five people employed at Studio 416. There was also a board of directors, but they weren't fully involved in the day-to-day operations. Interestingly, the gallery closed after Adam Walker entered politics.

"Someone has to know something," she said. "What happened to the other three people that worked there?"

Nick pulled up the research he did into Sharon's coworkers.

"Debbie Styles, the bookkeeper," Nick said as he pulled up her info. "She retired from the gallery after it closed. Nothing that raises any flags. But, lookie, lookie here."

"What?"

"Debbie Styles died in a car accident. About a year after Sharon disappeared," Nick said as his eyes scanned the text. "Lost control of her vehicle during a heavy storm and crashed head-on into a tree."

"Interesting," Ava mused. "What about the rest of them?"

Nick tapped on his computer as he pulled the data. All employees, except Adam Walker, were now dead due to various, seemingly unconnected reasons.

"What are the odds?" she mused. "Studio 416 must have been a very unlucky place to work. We need to talk to Adam Walker."

***

Adam Walker wasn't an easy man to find. Nick started looking into his whereabouts as soon as Ava hired him to be her assistant, but that proved to be quite a challenge. But he finally found him. Adam Walker was a resident in the Breezy Oaks retirement home, about an hour north of Toronto.

As they couldn't just waltz in and ask to speak to him, they devised a plan.

"Do you think this is going to work?" Nick asked as they drove up the tree-lined road.

"It will get us inside," she said. "Which is the best option we have for now."

Breezy Oaks was a sprawling estate with a large mansion that, according to the brochure, was built in the Edwardian Baroque revival Beaux-Arts style that was popular across Canada in the early twentieth century. It was designed for luxury, privacy and tranquillity. Today, it catered to those looking to place their loved ones in a secluded place with loads of privacy. Convenient if you wanted to hide from prying eyes.

"Not a bad place to hide," Nick said as he parked the Jeep in the small parking lot. "I bet you it's pricey."

"I think they present it as exclusive," she smiled as they got out of the car and made their way along the gavelled lot to the main building. "According to the website, this place was designed for entertaining. There is a conservatory, a great library and a bowling alley."

"Kinda has that Gatsby-esque vibe to it," he said. "I bet they have these fancy rooms with painted ceilings and pools with fountains."

"Wow, you've read the book?" she asked, surprised. "I didn't peg you as someone who would read Fitzgerald."

"I didn't," he winked at her. "But I did see the movie with Leonardo DiCaprio."

"Of course you did."

Their guide, Emily Levitt, was Breezy Oaks' no-nonsense director of operations and had kindly agreed to tour them around. Her face was a mask of politeness with a hint of practiced sympathy as they sat in her office.

"Thank you for seeing us on such short notice," Ava said as she took out a folded handkerchief out of her purse and dabbed her eyes. If Nick was surprised at the clipped British accent, he didn't let on. "I'm sorry, this is still so upsetting. My grandfather's condition will require personalized care, and this place came highly recommended."

"Of course, Ms Reed," Levitt replied. "We specialize in patients who require special care. I'm sure Breezy Oaks is the right place for your grandfather."

Ava dabbed her eyes again as she reached out for Nick's hand with all the drama she could muster. He took her hand, brought it up to his lips and kissed it lightly.

"Could we bother you for a glass of water, Ms Levitt?" Nick asked. "My fiancée is still very overwrought over what happened to Dr. Novak."

"Of course," Ms. Levitt smiled politely as she got up. "Just give me a moment."

They watched her leave the room. Ava got up and crossed the room to the neatly organized cabinets along the wall.

"I bet you this is where they keep the records," she whispered as she checked the drawers. "How long do you think we have before she comes back?"

"Not long," Nick said as he listened by the door. "Be quick about it. I'll try to stall her."

While Ave searched the cabinet, Nick met Ms Levitt outside as she was rushing back with the glass of water. He expertly blocked her way, so she was unable to see past him.

"May I have a quick word?" he asked, flashing her one of his charming smiles. She looked up at him breathlessly and nodded.

"You see, Ms Levitt," he glanced back towards her office as if he didn't want Ava to hear them and guided her away from the door. "My fiancée is extremely close to her grandfather. She wants to ensure that he gets the best care money can buy. Do you understand what I mean?"

She nodded several times, her eyes wide.

"We came here because we heard that Breezy Oaks is not only exclusive but also discreet," he purposely reached out and touched her shoulder. "Let's just say that Dr. Novak wants his privacy. You know what I'm saying?"

"Of course," Ms Levitt looked like she was about to down the glass of water herself. "Some of our clients are extremely exclusive. And, if the family wishes," she whispered. "We can ensure that their loved ones are kept extra comfortable. There are many medicines to ensure that."

"Good to hear, Ms Levitt," Nick said.

When they walked inside, Ava sat in her chair, dabbing her eyes. She took a small sip of the water and set the glass down on the desk.

"Do you think we can have that tour now?" she asked.

"Of course, Ms Reed."

***

The tour showed them the main parts of the building, including an impressive theatre room, ballroom and music room. They viewed a sample room to give them an idea of what her grandfather could expect.

"We have around-the-clock care on-premises," Ms. Levitt told them as she efficiently guided them through. "Our staff include doctors, nurses, physical therapists, nutritionists and other wellness staff."

So far, they haven't run into anyone that resembled Adam. Since it looked like they might be running out of places to see inside the buildings, Ava paused by the large window that looked over the manicured gardens.

"Look, darling," she said to Nick in her best Joan imitation. "What a charming garden."

"At Breezy Oaks, we believe that fresh air and regular exercise aid in the treatment of our patients," she said proudly. "Would you like to see the orangery?"

"An orangery," Ava said as Nick wrapped his arm around her waist. "How lovely."

"Lead the way, Ms Levitt," he said with a smile, ignoring Ava's elbow trying to push his arm away.

"What the hell are you doing?" she hissed at him.

"Trying to stay in character, darling," he said through his teeth as his hand slid further down just above her derriere. This was the most fun he had in a while.

The orangery was housed in a large glass greenhouse. It was full of lush trees and flowers with a small waterfront in the centre. There were several patients with their caregivers pushing them around down the paths. It was a bit creepy, in Ava's opinion, but she just smiled.

They were almost back at the house when the massive door opened, and a nurse brought out a man in a wheelchair. He was heavy set with silver-tipped hair and a dour expression on his round face.

As there was no way to get back in the building without passing them by, they waited for the nurse and her patient to pass by. The man in the wheelchair stared at Ava incredulously, and then he smiled.

"Sharon," he shouted. "SHARON."

"I'm sorry," she said. "I'm not…."

"Sharon," he said again, motioning to the nurse to stop. "What are you doing here? They said you were gone."

Ava leaned down, so she was face to face with the man while Nick stepped in front of Ms. Levitt to keep her from interfering.

"Gone?" Ava asked in a low voice as she crouched down beside him. "Gone where?"

"No," he shook his head suddenly. "That's not right."

"What's not right?"

"You're not Sharon," he said, his eyes filled with fear. "You can't be. They killed you. You're dead!"

"Who?" Ava asked. "Tell me."

The man suddenly became agitated, like a caged animal trying to get out. He kept screaming no, and it was clear she wasn't going to get any more information from him.

"I'm sorry," the nurse said, trying to calm him down as Ms. Levitt pushed around Nick.

"Nurse Dubner, take the patient somewhere more calming right away," she said before turning to Ava and Nick. "I'm sorry about that. Some of our patients are further gone than others. You should leave. I'll be happy to answer any additional questions you might have by email."

They said their goodbyes as Ms. Levitt almost pushed them out the door.

"What just happened?" Ava asked once they got back inside the Jeep.

"I think we found Adam Walker," Nick said. "Let's just hope nobody follows us after this visit."

"I found his file," she said. "He's definitely there. That man was almost unrecognizable. If he didn't mistake me for Sharon, we wouldn't have known that was him."

"They either pumped him up with drugs, or he has some serious health issues," Nick said. "Ms Levitt implied as much. For an extra charge, they can pump your loved one with enough drugs to keep them docile and cut off from the world."

"That's horrible," she whispered.

The drive home was uneventful. Whatever plans they had for working through the information they uncovered all fled away the moment they got back. As they walked up the walkway, Stan's door opened, and a tall man stepped out.

"Shit," she said under her breath. "That's my father."

"Ava," Michael came down the steps to greet her, his arms open wide for a hug. "We just got in. Figured we'd surprise you."

She let him hug her but didn't say a word, not ready to fully forgive him for his lies.

"You must be Nick," he said, extending his hand for a handshake. "Michael. We've heard so much about you."

"Nice to meet you." Nick shook Michael's hand, not reacting to the deliberate handshake and the warning look in the man's eyes. Sensing a family dispute in the making, he figured it would be easier to let them figure it out. "I'm sure I'll see you around."

"Why don't you come in," Michael said. "We ordered pizza. There is plenty to go around."

"Another time, perhaps," he said. "I'm sure you have lots to catch up on."

Ava watched him slither away. Traitor, she thought as she followed her father inside.

***

Ava woke up to the realization that her parents were here. The two people she didn't have time to deal with right now. Last night she updated them on Stan's condition, the investigation and her podcast. She decided to omit specific details, not wanting to worry them.

When she came downstairs, Joan was prancing around the kitchen like a fairy godmother.

"Good morning, darling," she smiled when Ava walked in. She reached over and lightly brushed the bangs from Ava's eyes. "Did you sleep well?"

"Yes," Ava said. "How about you?"

"It's jet lag. It gets me every time," Joan smiled. "I couldn't sleep, so I came down to make tea. Would you like some? There is coffee as well."

Ava opted for coffee. She filled up her mug, added sugar and sat down at the table. Joan did the same then set a plate filled with muffins on the table.

"We should talk," Joan said. "I know you're angry with your father."

"Can you blame me?" Ava said. "You both lied to me."

"Your father told me about your conversation," Joan continued. Her face pinched with concern. "With me, with both of us. And I know it sounds cliché, but we thought we were protecting you."

"By lying to me?"

"You were so little when Sharon went missing. It broke your father's heart to see you in so much pain. It didn't seem relevant at the time to tell you the truth about us," a vague ghost of a smile touched the corner of her lips. "Your father and I love each other. We always have. I can't and won't apologize for that."

"So why not just say that? Instead of lying."

"It was never that simple, Ava. I was married to another man. I broke my marriage vows to be with your father. We both knew it was wrong, but we couldn't help it," she shut her eyes at the memory. "I was so ashamed of what I've done. The affair could have ruined my marriage, your father's job, his career. So, I pushed him away."

"Did Sharon know?"

Joan took a sip of her tea before she answered.

"Sharon was a very astute young woman. But no, she didn't know. At least not at first," she set the cup down in front of her. "I'm sure you've already heard this. Sharon was intelligent, beautiful and charismatic. You couldn't help but be drawn to her. When I made the decision to break things off with Michael, he was so broken. Sharon was in his class, and she dazzled him. How could he resist her?

"I didn't blame him when they started dating, but it was killing me inside to see them together, knowing she could be with him when I couldn't. We ran into each other at a party. That's where that photo was taken. That night Sharon told me she was pregnant, and I knew I had lost him forever. I thought I was good at hiding my feelings, but she was smart. She found out the truth."

"What did she do?" Ava asked.

"She gave me an ultimatum," Joan said quietly, choosing her words carefully. "She told me to leave Michael alone and go back to my husband, or she was going to tell everyone about the affair. I had no choice but to leave. I couldn't let her ruin everything."

"Did Dad know about this?"

Tears shimmered in Joan's eyes as she shook her head. "I never told him, but I think he might have suspected something. Maybe she told him at some point. All I know is that when they started having problems and talking about divorce, he came to me. I couldn't turn him away again. Then my husband died, and the rest, you know."

Ava reached for Joan's hand and gave it a light squeeze. She was torn between her loyalty to the woman who gave her life and the one who raised her. "I'm sorry, Joan."

"You have nothing to be sorry about." Joan cradled Ava's cheek with her hand. I told you this to explain why we lied to you. Please don't blame your father for this. He loves you so very much. We both do."

"How can you?" Ava asked. "When I am so much like her. It must be so hard to look at me and not see her."

"Ah," Joan said knowingly. "I see what this is about. Darling, you might look like Sharon, but you're not just your mother's daughter. You are also your father's, and there is a lot of him inside you too," she smiled gently. "I thank Sharon every day for having you and for the privilege of being able to raise you. I wouldn't trade that for anything."

For the first time in her life, Ava realized that in all the time she spent looking for her mother, she overlooked the one she always had. The one who raised her and treated her as her own. The one who's always been there for her. Joan.

CHAPTER 14

"I got some information on Mitchell's property," Nick said as Ava walked into his living room. They temporarily set up the workspace in his parents' house if someone came looking for information again. Now with Joan and Michael as houseguests, this gave them space to work uninterrupted.

"Anything interesting?" she asked.

"Well, it might interest you that Mitchell and his wife bought the property for just under one million dollars back in 1998," Nick said. "That in itself doesn't seem significant."

"I sense a but," she said.

"You'd be right," he continued. "But, while a million dollars today is pretty much the average price of a home in Toronto, it wasn't so back then."

"So there goes the idea that Mitchell sold his house in the city and used the profit to buy the house in the country," Ava concluded. "Unless he was bringing home some serious money."

"It doesn't seem so," Nick shifted his chair over to give her room. "You see, just after Sharon went missing, the government started publishing an annual salary list for the highest earners in the public sector. The Sunshine List, as it's still called today, listed everyone making over one hundred thousand in salary annually."

"I take it that Frank Mitchell wasn't on that list," Ava guessed as she pulled up a chair and sat. "Back then, a hundred thousand was way more than it is today, no?"

"Significantly so," he agreed. "So that leads us back to the question of how does a cop on an average salary afford a house way out of his price range? He also retires early, meaning his pension wouldn't be as large as if he stayed the whole term."

"I'd say that unless he won the lottery or the money came from his wife, someone paid him off."

"It sure looks that way," Nick agreed. "And there is no way of asking him, now that he's dead.

"Again," Ava said. "Very convenient. I think I should pay Tyler another visit and see if we can swap updates."

"Is that all you gonna swap with Tyler?" he asked.

"Grow up," Ava rolled her eyes as she sent a quick email to Burnett.

She thought of the conversation she had with Joan earlier about Sharon. The picture her stepmother painted was still unclear.

"Do you believe in true love?" she asked suddenly.

"Ooh, are things getting serious with Tyler?" Nick asked with a raised eyebrow.

"What? No," she said. "This has nothing to do with him. It's about Sharon."

"You lost me."

"Remember when I said that I found out that my father was keeping certain information from me?" When he nodded, she continued. "It turns out that my father and Joan had an affair before Sharon."

"Lots of people have affairs," Nick said carefully. "What does it have to do with Sharon?"

"Well, they both said it was love, like deeply-rooted love that led to the affair. Joan was married at the time to my father's boss."

"Ouch."

"The affair would have ruined them all. Joan, my father, his boss. So she broke it off with him." Ava paused, trying to figure out how she felt about this. "My father was Sharon's teaching assistant. After Joan dumped him, he and Sharon got together."

Ava grabbed her bag and pulled out the picture she found of all of them together.

"I found this picture. They are all in it," she gave it to Nick to see. "Anyway, Sharon found out. Threatened to expose the affair unless Joan backed off and went back to her husband."

"Understandable," Nick said as he gave her back the picture. "Can you blame her?"

"I don't," Ava said. "I probably would have done the same. But they got back together anyway. My father and Joan. After her husband died. That's why my parents divorced."

"Do you think they had something to do with her death?" he asked.

"No," she said. "But I think this gives me a clearer picture of who Sharon was. She wasn't as nice and easy-going as everyone seems to believe."

"Would you be nice if your husband had an affair with an old lover?"

"It's not that," Ava said. "It's hard to explain, but I don't think she cared that much about my father. She demanded things in the divorce but didn't want him."

"So, what does that mean?"

"I'm starting to think she was definitely capable of blackmail. She was brash, arrogant, and that's what got her killed."

***

Nick considered her words.

"So you think the records we found are proof that she was blackmailing someone?"

"Yes and no," she said. "I think that, yes, Sharon was capable of blackmail if she thought she could get what she wanted. Did she want money? Maybe. But she was smart. If she was blackmailing someone, she would have original copies of the accounts, not copies. I also don't think she would keep those electronically."

"You think she would have had physical records with names and the incriminating information?"

"Yes. That's why I still think she found something and used it as leverage. It was like a game to her," Ava said excitedly. "Yes, everyone agreed that she was brilliant. Some described her as selfish, ruthless and persistent. Others insisted she could do no wrong. So, which one was it?"

"Maybe she was both," Nick suggested. "People can be both ruthless and charismatic."

"I think we should plant some information online," Ava suggested. "People are always asking questions in the online forums and chat rooms. I haven't provided many updates, but maybe it's time."

"That could be dangerous," he pointed out. "Remember what happened when we didn't announce what we found?"

"You can always back out of a job," she said. "I will fully understand."

"Oh please," Nick rolled his eyes. "I live for excitement."

"That's what I like to hear," Ava smiled at him. "Now, let's do some more digging and plan out what we will leak."

Ava's phone buzzed as a message came in.

"Stan's awake," she said excitedly. "I have to go to the hospital."

"I'll drive."

Michael and Joan were already at the hospital when Ava and Nick arrived. She rushed into the room. Stan looked pale. He was hooked up to machines, but he was awake and talking. Feeling relieved, she rushed to his side.

"Oh, Grandpa," she said as she grabbed his hand and squeezed it. "I was so worried about you."

Stan touched her cheek and smiled. "It takes a bit more than a knock on the head to take me out." He pointed to his head and said proudly, "It's hard as a rock."

"Now, Stan," Michael said. "You were lucky Ava found you when she did. This could have ended up very differently."

"But it didn't, Dad," Ava said. "Let's not dwell on that."

Michael shook his head in frustration but let it go.

"The doctors said you'll need physiotherapy," he said. "We could get an occupational therapist to come to the house to help with the recovery. You definitely can't stay alone at the house until you're better."

"I won't be alone," Stan said. "I have Ava."

"We could stay for a while longer," Joan chimed in. "Until you get better. Ava has a lot of stuff on her plate right now."

"Oh, no, dear," Stan quickly reassured her. "That won't be necessary. Honestly."

"I can stay with Grandpa," she told them. She would stay as long as he wanted her to.

Everyone had an opinion on the best arrangement but couldn't reach a consensus. Nick watched the scene with amusement. Joan was fussing over Stan and calming her husband as Ava explained how she would take care of her grandfather.

"I can't believe how stubborn you are, Stan," Michael said in frustration.

"I'm not stubborn," Stan insisted. "I'm a grown man. I don't need to be treated like a child."

"Really now?" Michael said mockingly. "You can't even stay home alone right now. I swear, stubbornness runs in this whole family. It's like arguing with a rock sometimes."

"You aren't always as reasonable as you think you are, darling," Joan said with a twinkle in her eyes that made Ava laugh.

"I can definitely think of a place," Nick told Ava when they were out of earshot. "They might already be expecting a call about Dr. Novak."

"Oh god," Ava shrugged. "I'd never put anyone in that place. It's like a Victorian asylum. I wouldn't be surprised if they had torture rooms in the basement."

"I wouldn't put it past them," Nick laughed. "How did you come up with Dr. Novak anyway?

"Well, he is a doctor, "she winked. "Just one of those PdD ones. They didn't ask for clarification."

They stayed with Stan for a while longer, arguing over whose suggestion was best, but couldn't reach a compromise. When the nurse finally came in, signalling the end of the visit, they all agreed to sleep on it.

***

"I can't believe you managed to get inside Breezy Oaks," Tyler adjusted his tie as he listened. "It's a private facility with very tight security."

"We weren't trespassing," Ava assured him. "I called ahead and made an appointment to see the palace. I told them my grandfather was in a hospital recovering from a brain injury, and I needed a place for him ASAP. That's not a lie."

"Maybe not, but it could have ended differently if you were caught," he pointed out.

"But we didn't," she pointed out. "Plus, now we know Adam Walker is in there. I think he might be drugged."

She opened her bag and took out several printouts, and handed them over.

"I took pictures of his file," she said. "He is supposed to be suffering from dementia, but they are giving him a lot of strange drugs."

Tyler looked over the papers. "You know this is highly problematic."

"Yes," she agreed. "I think they are purposely keeping him sedated."

"No," Tyler clarified. "You broke into confidential patient files without permission."

"Oh, yeah."

"I did not see this," Tyler shoved the papers back at her. "You never told me about this. But, I will go see Mr. Walker and have a conversation with him."

Ava smiled at him. "Do you have any updates on Sharon's case?"

"Yes and no," Tyler said as she put the printouts away. "We got some information on the accounts Sharon had on the floppy disks. They look like two sets of books. The notes in her notebook corresponded with some of the names in the accounts. Those are of various shell corporations and offshore bank accounts."

"Is that what she took pictures of as well?" Ava asked.

"Yes," Tyler confirmed. "It would suggest Sharon took pictures as a backup. It's taking some time to figure out who owned the numbered corporations. Some of them don't even exist anymore."

"So she could have set them up?" Ava asked. "The offshore accounts and shell corporations?"

"It's possible. But that takes time and resources. But, since many of them were set up before Sharon even stepped foot in

Studio 416, it doesn't look like she had anything to do with that."

"In her notebook, Sharon made notes of what looked like names and dates besides the amounts. Was that a list of people she had something on, or was it proof there was something shady going on at the gallery?"

"Look, it's possible she uncovered something she wasn't supposed to," Tyler said. "There are patterns, initials and dates. Lots of money flowing back and forth. Sharon noted which accounts showed large transfers. Some had question marks beside some, exclamation points by others."

"You said two sets of books," Ava said. "Does that mean she was the one fixing the accounts? Could she have been funnelling the money from different accounts for her personal use?"

"It definitely would have been very easy for her to keep two sets of books without anyone knowing," Tyler said. "Sharon was either a clever embezzler, a blackmailer or a whistleblower that discovered something she shouldn't have."

"Does that bring us any closer to finding answers?"

"It gives us new avenues to tug on," Tyler said. "But there is something else."

Tyler grabbed one of the files on his desk and took out the report he wanted to show her.

"What's this?" she asked.

"The forensics lab finally came through," he explained. "Whoever broke in and attacked Stan left his DNA behind. We ran it through our data system and got a match. Does the name Anthony Lowell mean anything to you?"

"I don't think so," Ava said, trying to jog her memory. "Do you have a picture?"

Tyler opened the folder and took out the photograph, and placed it in front of her.

Ava stared at the man in the photograph. She'd seen this face before. But where?

"I have seen this picture before," she said slowly as the memory came back. "When I was leaving Halifax, there was a story about a man whose body was fished out of the Halifax harbour. I'm pretty sure this was the man."

"Are you sure?" Tyler's pulse quickened.

"Yes, but how could he have broken into the house when he's been dead for over a decade?"

"The man we're looking for is Anthony Lowell's son," Tyler said. "The only problem is that Anthony Lowell never existed before he was found in the harbour."

"Do you think he could have killed Sharon?" Ava asked. "Did someone kill him?"

"According to the reports from the Halifax police. Anthony Lowell, or whoever he was, most likely ended up in the water accidentally," he told her. "The car slid off the road and plunged into the icy waters where he sat on the bottom of the Harbour for a few years before amateur scuba divers found him.

"That sure changes things, "Ava said. "Can I have a copy of that picture? I have an idea."

***

While Nick searched for the elusive Anthony Lowell and his connection to Sharon, Ava shifted her focus to the upcoming season of The Missing Voices. The following season would feature several cases in and around Calgary before they moved on to Colorado.

Now, she was on a call with Lori and Beth Draker, an investigative reporter working in Calgary who would provide local perspective for the new season of the podcast.

Beth was a short woman with a big personality who knew how to sniff out a story. Lori has been in contact with her for some time as they worked on selecting stories to feature. As a crime beat reporter, Beth was their go-to source for information on the ground, and she jumped at the opportunity to keep these stories on the minds of as many people as she could.

"I want you to know that it wasn't easy for me to select cases for your podcast," Beth said as they worked out their game plan. "There are too many families out there with missing loved ones, and they all deserve answers."

She tucked a piece of her dark hair behind her ear and tapped her pen on the desk. "I've worked with several outlets in the past to help amplify these stories with mixed results. Some people are just more interested in sensationalizing them for their own entertainment rather than telling the stories."

"We're not like that," Ava said. She really liked Beth and her dedication to the cases she covered. "We're here to tell those stories hoping they will bring some answers for the families. I know the pain they feel. I know what it's like to live in limbo, looking for answers."

"I know, and that's why I am very excited to work with you," Beth said. "I've been listening to your podcast for some time now, and I'm familiar with your mom's case. I'm sorry that she's not coming back as you hoped."

"Thank you," Ava said.

"Did finding her make things easier for you to deal with what happened?"

"Not really. I hoped it would, but," Ava paused as if trying to find the right words." "When they are missing, you have hope. It's a long shot, but there is a part of you that hopes they will one day walk through that door. Then when you find out that they are not coming back, it's like losing them all over again. It rips you apart. I don't know what's worse. Believing that my mother stole money and left me or the fact that she's been dead all this time and I've spent most of my life hating her."

She thought about it while the other two women sat in silence.

"You know, I don't remember her," Ava told them, momentarily lost in thought as she played with her pendant. "She's a total stranger. Growing up, I was so angry with her for leaving. I wanted to find her just so I could tell her how much I hated her. Then I found out she never left."

"You don't have to talk about it," Beth told her.

"No, it's fine," Ava said. "I am not angry with her anymore. I just want to find out who did this. The person who took her away from me and stole my memories."

"I really hope you do," Beth said and looked from Ava to Lori and back. "I'm sure you've probably already thought about this, but this could be a great topic for a whole season of The Missing Voices."

"Oh, we've already talked about this," Lori said with a smile. "Many people want to hear the story, so we'll definitely look at Sharon's case in detail."

"Hopefully, you'll get more answers soon," Beth said sincerely. "I'm sure you're doing a lot of work on this already. All right, back to why we're here."

After several minutes, Ava agreed. Beth was right—there were too many families still looking for answers. More often than not, they never got them. Every case was always a battle between fascination and outrage. Not all victims were treated with equal respect. How many cases went unsolved because someone didn't deem them worthy enough to investigate? Too many. Time went by, evidence was lost, and the victims were forgotten. This part always pissed Ava off.

That's why she always tried to focus on the things that could make a difference. Ava loved puzzles. Trying to figure out the missing pieces was always the most intriguing part. The clues left behind didn't always make sense, especially when you looked at them individually. But pushed together, they formed a picture. Sometimes it was too vague to make sense. Other times, there were too many clues that distracted instead of providing clarity.

They went over evidence, mapped out suitable locations and drafted the storylines. They re-read available statements, scheduled appointments to interview families and investigators.

They meticulously compiled pictures, social profiles, and other information about the victims they could get their hands on for each case. The older cases were always more complex as not all families had many pictures of their loved ones. Often those pictures were the only memories they had left.

Ava's thoughts went to the picture of Sharon sitting on her desk. The 1995 Sharon would forever be ingrained in her mind, no matter how old she got. The world moved on, yet she stayed the same. Over the years, she saw so many pictures of the missing and the dead. Every one of them, frozen in time. How many of them never made their way home?

CHAPTER 15

Solving cases was sometimes like making wine. First, you had to plant the vines and wait for the grapes to grow before you could even start harvesting them. Yes, the wine-making process was a long one, entirely dependent on the elements and experience. And patience.

Tyler was a patient man. In his line of work, he had to be. Murder was never easy, but solving the cold ones was even more challenging. Lucky for him, he liked a challenge, and he had a knack for sticking his nose in places he shouldn't have.

Once he knew where to find Adam Walker, he managed to arrange a visit. While the administrators at Breezy Oaks didn't take kindly to his request, they couldn't deny him either. Whether they like it or not, Adam Walker was part of an investigation into the murder of Sharon Novak, his former employee.

The visit was arranged with a condition. He could interview Walker with his caregiver, Nurse Dubner, present to monitor the patient's health. As they sat in the large games room, Tyler could hardly believe that the man before him was the same Adam Walker. The man who seemingly disappeared from public view over a decade ago, was almost unrecognizable.

"Hello, Mr. Walker," he started. "My name is Detective Tyler Burnett."

Adam looked at him with a surprisingly clear gaze. Nurse Dubner watching him like a hawk. Tyler wasn't sure he was going to get anywhere.

"You can call me Adam," he said slowly and looked into the distance.

"Thank you for seeing me," Tyler continued. "I'm here because I'm investigating the murder of Sharon Novak. Can you help me, Adam?"

"Sharon," he said absently. "Beautiful, clever Sharon."

"She worked for you. Do you remember her?"

"One doesn't forget someone like Sharon," he smiled absently. "So smart."

"What else can you tell me about her?" Tyler asked, keeping his voice steady.

"Sharon," Adam repeated her name. "She's like a breath of fresh air."

"Adam," Tyler said again, trying to get him to focus. "Sharon found something she shouldn't have. Didn't she?"

Adam looked over, startled. Tyler wasn't sure if he pushed too hard.

"I told her to let it go," he said, looking away again. "She didn't listen. I begged her to stop."

"Stop what?"

"She's going to be mad," Adam's voice was almost a whisper. "She's going to hurt me. I don't want her to hurt me."

"It's okay, Adam," Tyler said gently. "I won't let her hurt you."

There was silence again. Tyler debated how much further he could push him before he went too far.

"Sharon," Adam said again, looking over at Tyler. "I saw her here. She was here."

"Sharon is dead," Tyler said, his voice gentle yet firm. "Someone hurt Sharon, Adam. Do you know who hurt her?"

"But I saw her," he insisted. "Sharon was here. Her hair was different, but it was her. I know it was her." He stared into the distance. "She was here. I saw her."

"Adam," Tyler said. "Look at me."

Adam Walker, the man who once wielded tremendous power and had the world at his feet, looked at him like a petulant child being scolded for pinching some candy. His pale eyes, trying to focus.

"Sharon is dead. Someone killed her," Tyler said. "The woman you saw was her daughter."

"Her daughter?" he asked with confusion in his eyes.

"Yes, Sharon's daughter, Ava," Tyler said. "She wants to know who killed her mother, Adam. Do you know who hurt Sharon?"

Adam nodded but refused to say anything else. Tears suddenly appeared in his eyes.

"Sharon," he said again. "Beautiful, clever Sharon."

Adam started to repeat himself. He alternated between staring into the distance and trying not to cry.

"Adam," Tyler said again. "Tell me who killed Sharon?"

"I'm sorry," Adam whispered. "I told her to let it go."

Adam started to cry softly, and Tyler rubbed his forehead in frustration.

"That's enough, Detective," the nurse told him. "You're upsetting him"

"I need to show him something," Tyler said. "It'll be just a moment."

He placed the picture of Anthony Lowell in front of Adam's face.

"Do you recognize this man?" he asked.

There was a flash of recognition followed by another one that looked like fear.

"Where did you get this?" he whispered.

"It doesn't matter," Tyler said. "Tell me about him. The man in the picture."

Adam's mouth moved, but no sounds came out. He kept staring at the photo, his face filled with panic. Suddenly he reached for Tyler's arm. Gripped it.

"You have to find Sharon," he said in a raspy whisper. "Tell her to stop. Stop looking," he swallowed hard, his eyes wide. "Sharon. SHARON."

"That's enough. You need to leave," she ordered, then called for assistance.

***

As Tyler was escorted out of the building, Adam Walker was taken back to his room and given sedatives to calm him down. As Adam was staring out the window, he didn't notice a man disguised as one of the staff slip into his room.

The man closed the door and walked up to Adam's bed.

"What are you doing here?" Adam shrieked, his eyes wide.

"Shut up, old man," the voice was low and sharp, the eyes cold and cruel. "You never learn, do you?"

"Please, don't hurt me," he said.

"I said shut up. You were supposed to keep your fucking mouth shut."

"But she was here," he trembled. "Sharon was here."

"That stupid bitch has been dead for the last two decades. Don't you remember?" he laughed. "She's dead because of you."

"No," Adam's eyes tried to focus. "That can't be right. I saw her."

"Sharon Novak is dead," the man's eyes went flat. "And now, it's your turn."

Adam's eyes darted toward the emergency button in his room as he reached out to signal for help. But he was too slow. The panic that filled him now shook his whole body. He tried to scream, but no sound came out.

The man slapped him hard. Before he knew what was happening, there was darkness around him. He couldn't breathe. As Adam fought for his life, his killer pressed the pillow over his face waiting for him to die.

He held it there until Adam's body finally went limp. For good measure, he held it there for another moment before removing it from the lifeless body.

He tucked the pillow under the dead man's head as if it's always been there. For good measure, he searched the room for anything that shouldn't be there. He searched the drawers on the side table and in the closet. A quick search through the pockets didn't reveal anything useful.

Not finding anything incriminating, he left Adam in his bed as he slipped out of the room. Before he closed the door behind him, Adam's killer gave him one more disgusted look. Why couldn't people just do what they were told?

The killer was familiar with the layout of the building and the many passages reserved for staff to seamlessly move around without disturbing the patients. Disguised as one of them, he made his way out of the building. Nobody stopped him, nor did they ask any questions. It was almost too easy.

It wouldn't be long before Adam's body was discovered. He smiled as he imagined the panicked nurses running down the hallway, wondering what had happened. They wouldn't be able to help him, no matter how hard they tried. It was too late.

He made his way into one of the nearby buildings, where he changed back into his clothes. Dressed in black, his hair covered by a dark ball cap, he walked out and didn't stop. When he was a safe distance away, he pulled out the phone and dialled a familiar number.

"It's done," he said and then disappeared into the trees.

It didn't take long before Adam's body was found by his nurse, who raised the alarm. The police were notified right after, and so was Detective Burnett.

While Tyler played the scene in his head repeatedly, wondering if he could have gotten more out of Adam if pushed, he got the call from Breezy Oaks. He turned his car around and drove back.

He definitely didn't anticipate this turn of events.

***

"I got you something," Nick said as he handed Ava a small white bag. He shoved his hands in his pockets as she took the bag from him.

"You got me a gift?" she said, surprised. "Wait, are you getting sweet on me now?"

"If I was sweet on you, you'd know," he said with a suggestive look. "Just open it."

She took out a small box, about the size of her palm. Inside was a small white object, about a square inch in size. It was smooth on one side and decorated with a spiral swirl across the other. A small, silver loop topped one of the edges.

"You got me a keychain?" Ava asked as she took it out of the box and examined it. It looked delicate but felt quite sturdy to the touch. She ran her finger over the smooth surface and realized the loop was actually a clip.

"It's not a keychain," Nick said impatiently. "It's like a personal safety alert device. You clip it on your key, clothes, jewellery, purse, whatever. I figured it was small enough so that you can attach it to many different things. Most women have all kinds of things like that, so I figured you do too."

"Aww, Nick, you got me a panic button?" she smiled. "You are sweet on me."

For a brief moment, he actually looked embarrassed. "Don't be ridiculous."

"How does it work?"

"You have to download the app and create an account," he explained. "It has several options where you can enter up to three emergency contacts. You press the button once if you feel unsafe, and it alerts them to call you. If you press and hold, it connects to the monitoring system that alerts the police. Check the instructions. You'll figure it out."

"Thank you," she said. "That's very thoughtful."

"Yeah, well," he said and sat down at the desk. "I figured you could use one since you always seem to get into dangerous situations. Now, can we move on?"

Ava put the button back in the box and set it on the desk. She would set it up later.

"Sure, did you find anything new?"

"I did some more research on Studio 416," Nick said. "I had to go through a lot of sites to find something useful. The gallery was established by George Elliot Northam, Elizabeth's father, to support local artists and promote artistic expression. It was largely funded by the NorFast Group."

"Interesting," Ava said as she looked at the screen over Nick's shoulder. "I thought it was common for large companies to support various non-profits."

"Support, yes," he said. "But Studio 416 was only funded by the NorFast Group. There were donors and wealthy clients, but NorFast was the main backer behind it."

"Perhaps George started the gallery to give his stepson something to do. Why not and get in a few nice tax breaks while at it?"

"That's pretty generous for any parent," Nick said. "Even more so for a stepfather."

"Studio 416 closed not long after Sharon went missing," Ava noted as she read the notes. "Adam's career shifted to politics after that. That's a bit of an odd shift. From a gallery to politics?"

"It seems his heart was more set on art than it was on the corporate world. According to his bio - it's still online, by the way - he got a degree in fine arts. I tried to find some of his works, but nothing stood out. Average student, mediocre artist."

"And a daddy with deep pockets. Why bother getting your foot in the door when you can just get your own door and everything else that comes with it?" Ava walked over to the couch and sat down. "I wonder how the daughter, Elizabeth, felt about this."

"Based on the bio on the company site," he read. "Elizabeth went to the best schools and graduated at the top of her class with degrees in business and finance. She'd worked for the family business from an early age and took over the reins upon her father's death."

"So the gallery probably wasn't her thing then," Ava mused. "Does she have any kids?"

"Not that I can find. She never posts anything to suggest that on the few social media sites she uses. In general, her online presence is limited."

They both studied the woman's face on his computer screen. Nick swirled the chair around to face Ava. He stretched out his legs and crossed them at the ankles.

"I'd say she got a better deal," he said. "Daddy might have opened the gallery for Adam, but the real moneymaker went to her. She got the company, the name and the money."

"Yeah, I agree," Ava said. "I don't think she spent too much time crying about it."

"She doesn't strike me as a crier."

"Definitely not," Ava laughed. "Did you find anything on the guy from the Harbour? Anthony Lowell?"

"Not exactly," Nick went back to the computer. "I found something even better. Check this out."

"Wow," Ava said in surprise. "What do we have here?"

***

She stared at the man's face on the screen. He had the same face and similar hair to the man pulled out of the Halifax waters. His eyes stared right at the camera. But his name wasn't Anthony Lowell. It was Antonio DiPalma.

"Who the heck is Antonio DiPalma?" she asked.

"That is an excellent question," Nick said. "I found the name when I was looking at Studio 416, but that was before you sent me the info on Anthony Lowell. I didn't put the two and two together at first because I wasn't looking for him."

"Did he work at the gallery then?" Ava asked. "I don't remember his name in any interviews or reports."

"He didn't technically work at Studio 416. It was more like he did work for them," Nick pulled up the information. "The gallery mainly sold and exhibited art. They also worked with local artists to help them gain exposure. Antonio DiPalma was one of those artists."

"He must have known Sharon then," Ava's hand automatically reached for her pendant. "Was he there long?"

"It seems that Antonio DiPalma was almost exclusively featured at the gallery in and around the time of Sharon's disappearance," Nick said. "Other than the gallery, there wasn't a lot of information available on DiPalma online. What's there is pretty dated."

"Not surprising," she said. "Considering that he was dead before the Internet took off mainstream. Did you find any more pictures?"

"I thought you'd never ask," Nick smiled and pulled up the pages to show her.

She saw it then, right there in front of her. Sharon and other coworkers with DiPalma at the gallery. In one of the pictures, it was just Sharon and DiPalma looking very cozy.

"So they knew each other," she said. "Probably quite well. Why doesn't his name appear in any reports?"

"Another excellent question, and one I can't answer," Nick told her. "But take a look at some of his art that was featured at the gallery."

Antonio DiPalma fancied himself as a young Pablo Picasso even if he lacked the talent. His works included paintings, sculptures, ceramics and metalwork. They were prominently displayed at Studio 416 and even sold for reasonable amounts of money.

"You know, I would never claim to be an art expert," she said. "But, I've spent enough time in museums and grand palaces where the rich made a hobby out of collecting art. I don't think DiPalma was very good."

"I'd agree. See here?" Nick pointed at one of the pictures with some of DiPalma's art. "There is more to a painting than just what's in it. Sure, you need composition, colours and the right focal point, but there is also technique. Artists can quickly bring out emotions and impact the viewers with simple brush strokes and colour choices. He doesn't quite get that. It lacks heart."

"So, for someone with seemingly no talent, being featured exclusively at an established gallery must have been quite the feat," she said. "But why? Surely they could find better artists. How profitable could selling mediocre art be?"

"If Sharon's records were from the gallery, then I would say very."

"So not only were they selling mediocre art, someone was willing to pay a lot of money for it," she touched the pendant as she spoke. "Unless it wasn't about art. Or, at least not this particular art."

"What do you mean?"

"Sharon wasn't an artist, but she would have grown up with art, especially the classics. Like I did," Ava said. "She would definitely question why something so ordinary would be selling for such a great amount of money."

"Here is what I don't understand," Nick said. "Everyone kept saying how smart Sharon was and how good she was with numbers. If you have something shady going on at the gallery, why hire her in the first place knowing she could become a threat?"

"Maybe they hired her as an asset," Ava said. "She was a wiz with computers and numbers. I bet someone with her skill set would be very attractive at that time, especially if you wanted to hide something."

"Do you hire her hoping she sees things your way, or does she go in knowing exactly what is going on, and then for some reason, turns against you?"

"It could have gone down either way," Ava thought. "Once Sharon stopped being an asset, she became a liability. She knew enough to make her dangerous. Nervous enough to see her as a threat. One that had to be eliminated."

CHAPTER 16

Tyler decided to have another chat with Elizabeth Northam, and this time, it was going to be on his turf. Instead of going to her, he made a formal request for her to come into the station. He knew she wouldn't like that, and he was right.

Elizabeth showed up with her lawyer, dressed in a slick black suit that probably cost more than he made in a month. The lawyer, equipped with a leather case, a no-nonsense attitude and a hint of annoyance, made it very clear this interview was a waste of his client's time.

This time, Tyler made her wait. She was used to giving orders and having people wait on her all the time. He hoped reversing those roles would throw her off just enough to slip up. She knew something, and he needed to know what it was.

"This is outrageous," the lawyer spat out as soon as Tyler walked in. "You're wasting my client's valuable time with this ridiculous interview."

Tyler nodded as if acknowledging the complaint. He then looked directly at Elizabeth.

"Ms Northam," he said. "I appreciate you coming in, especially during this difficult time. Your brother's death must have come as a shock."

Elizabeth gave a slight nod in acknowledgement. He saw no grief in those piercing blue eyes. Her mouth tightened in a firm line with a touch of irritation just around the corners.

"Adam's death was unfortunate," she said, never taking her eyes off him. "But I fail to see what that has to do with me being here."

"I believe that your brother's death is connected to Sharon Novak's murder," Tyler said. "The woman who worked for your brother and whose body was found on your site."

"My client has already answered your questions about that woman," the lawyer chimed in. "A woman who was employed by my client's brother, not her, over two decades ago."

"And yet, your client has a connection to both the woman, Sharon Novak," Tyler emphasized her name again, "and the location where Sharon's body was found."

"It's a coincidence," the lawyer said. "Nothing links my client directly to that woman and what happened to her. Are we done here?"

"Not quite," Tyler said. He opened his file folder, took out a picture of the man fished out of the Halifax harbour. "Ms Northam, are you familiar with a man by the name of Anthony Lowell?"

He saw the flash of surprise in her eyes. Her gaze lingered on the photo just a bit longer than necessary.

"I don't," she said, but this time her voice wasn't as controlled.

"What about Antonio DiPalma?"

"My client doesn't know these men, Detective," this time it was the lawyer who answered as he pushed the photo back towards Tyler. "I fail to see what this has to do with my client. Did these men have something to do with that woman's death?'

Tyler didn't answer him. Instead, he opened the folder again and pulled out the picture of Sharon and DiPalma that Ava sent him. He placed it in front of Elizabeth.

She stared at it with surprise. Her fingers itched to touch it and pull it closer, but she didn't. Something flashed across her face when she looked at it, but she hid it well. When she looked up and met Tyler's gaze, her face was impassive.

"What is this?" she asked.

"This is Sharon Novak with Antonio DiPalma," Tyler said, watching her expression. "He was an artist featured at Studio 416. The gallery your brother ran. Surely you would have met him?"

For a moment, it looked like she was going to say something but didn't. She tilted her head and looked him straight in the eye. "I couldn't say."

Tyler took the photo and placed it back in his folder. Elizabeth stared at it as if hoping to see the contents.

"Can you tell me you were when your brother died?" Tyler asked suddenly.

"My client doesn't have to answer that," the lawyer protested.

"I was in meetings," she answered at the same time. "In my office. I'm sure that's already been verified."

"Do you know who would have wanted your brother dead?"

"I would think that as a former politician, Adam probably made many enemies," she said. "Like I already told you, we weren't close."

"I think we're done here," the lawyer stood up and grabbed his case. "If there is anything else, you can contact my office directly."

Tyler watched them leave. People like her always demanded answers, especially when they felt inconvenienced. He showed her two photos with the same man without specifying his name.

Her lawyer referred to two men as if he didn't know they were the same person. Tyler didn't correct him, and Elizabeth didn't ask for clarification either.

She also never inquired about the progress of the investigation into her brother's death. Either she really didn't care or already knew who was responsible, just like she knew that DiPalma and Lowell were the same person. Tyler was sure she was hiding something, and she was connected to Sharon's murder. Now he had to figure out how.

***

When Ava got home from the gym, she didn't expect to find Stan and her parents waiting for her. They all sat around the living room having tea and cookies. She leaned against the doorway as she watched them.

"Isn't this lovely," she said. "Are we having brunch or something?"

"Oh good, you're here, Ava," Stan motioned for her to join them. He was still pale but seemed more like himself. "Come sit."

"What's going on?" she asked.

"I've been doing a lot of thinking," he said. "I think I want to sell the house."

"What do you mean?" Ava looked at her grandfather, puzzled. "Why would you want to sell the house?"

"I'm getting too old to maintain this place," he said slowly. "It's too much of a house for an old man like me."

"But I'm here," she said. "I can help you take care of the house."

Stan nodded his head and smiled.

"You have your own life, Ava, and it's not about living here with your grandfather," he raised his hand as if to stop her from arguing. "Truth be told, I'm tired. I'm tired of living in the past. I want to spend whatever is left of my life actually enjoying it."

"What do you mean?" Ava asked with a sinking feeling in her belly.

"I stayed in this house hoping that one day your mother would come back. I didn't want her to return and wonder what happened to us. To think we gave up on her," he glanced around the room filled with photographs and personal mementos. "Now that she's not coming back, I don't need to hold on to this place."

"Did you know about this?" Ava asked her parents.

"Stan mentioned it to us a few days ago," Michael said as he set his cup and saucer on the table. "We support his decision."

"It's still not set in stone," Stan told her. "I wanted to talk to you about it first."

"You don't have to ask my permission, Grandpa," she said. "This is your home."

"It's also yours," he said. "I don't want you to think that I'm giving up on Sharon or taking your memories away."

She walked over to where he sat and crouched beside him. The fact that he didn't want to sell the house without telling her first touched her. This was her connection to Sharon, but maybe it was time for them all to let go.

"I think that's a great idea, Grandpa," she smiled at him. "But where would you go?"

"I've had my eye on several very nice retirement residences," Stan said. "I haven't decided which one yet, but there is time."

"Please don't tell me one of those options is Breezy Oaks."

"What's Breezy Oaks?" Stan asked, confused.

"Never mind," she smiled. "Tell me about this palace you're looking at."

"I got a lead on this retirement home from one of my friends," Stan said. "Think of it as a condominium by the water-filled with all kinds of amenities but for retired people. A place where I can socialize with others my age and do all the things I do anyway."

"Sounds like fun," Ava said. She couldn't fault Stan for wanting to be around people his age. Doing ordinary things other people did that didn't revolve around the dead. The more she thought about it, the more she liked the idea. He could use some companionship when she wasn't around.

"We were thinking of driving down to see some places," Joan told her. "You are welcome to join us."

"Maybe I should start looking for a place of my own," Ava smiled.

"You'll always have a home with us," Michael assured her. "For as long as you want. And if one day you decide to get a place of your own, we'll support that decision no matter where it is."

"Thanks, Dad," she smiled at him then looked back at Stan. "I think this is a great idea, Grandpa. I would love to see this retirement home with you."

She hoped it was nothing like Breezy Oaks. That place gave her the creeps. Something weird was going on there, but she couldn't place her finger on what that was. She would do everything in her power to keep her grandfather out of such a place.

***

Nick got home later than he expected. He spent the day doing a photo shoot for a client that had a new line of sportswear. It was great fun, but it also took up a large chunk of his time. Afterwards, he met up with Steve and a few friends for a drink and now all he wanted was a shower.

The rain came down just as he was parking on the street. He grabbed the cases with his equipment out of the trunk and carried them to the house as he got soaked on the way. Nick swore under his breath as he got to the door. At least the porch was covered, but now he had to search around for his house key while everything stuck to him.

"Hey," he turned at the sound of Ava's voice. She sat in one of the chairs with her legs curled under her as she played on her phone. She wore sweats and a long sleeve shirt that slid slightly off her right shoulder, exposing a thick bright strap of her tank top. Unlike him, she was dry and comfortable.

"I didn't see you there," Nick said. "What, no hot date tonight?"

She took the headphones out of her ears and smiled.

"Not tonight," she said. "Dad and Joan went out to dinner, and Grandpa is sleeping. I thought I'd sit here and enjoy the rain."

"Want some company?" he asked, surprising himself.

"Sure," she said. "I'll be here."

Nick got the cases inside and went straight upstairs. Fifteen minutes later, he came back out in dry clothes. Just like Ava, he went for sweats and a t-shirt. He felt human again as he joined her.

"I uploaded the bits and pieces about Studio 416 and Antonio DiPalma to the forums and your site," he told her. "Hopefully, someone will come forward with something useful."

"Hopefully," Ava said, then added, "Burnett said someone killed Adam Walker."

"What?" he asked. "When?"

"Burnett went to see him," Ave said as she filled him in on what happened.

"I don't like it," Nick said. "Too many dead bodies keep turning up. Did you set up your panic button?"

"I did," she said. "I set you up as one of my emergency contacts for now."

"Let's hope you don't have to use it."

Ava smiled. This new Grumpy Nick was a lot more fun than Smug Nick. She definitely didn't expect him to get her the panic button. It was a nice gesture, so she decided to try being nicer to him too.

"Stan is thinking of selling the house," she said.

Nick nodded. There was no reason to tell her that he already knew that.

"How do you feel about it?"

"Good, I think," she said. "It was weird at first when he told me. But the more I thought about it, the more sense it made. This house has too many memories for all of us."

"What are you going to do?"

"I don't know. For the first time in my life, I don't have a plan," she admitted. "My whole life had one purpose. To find Sharon. I hadn't planned what I would do once I did."

"Are you going to move back to London?" he asked. The idea didn't sit well with him, but he kept it to himself.

"I'm thinking of finding a place here in Toronto," she said. "That way, I can be close to Stan and have a permanent base to work out of. My parents' house in London is great, but I think I'm ready for my own space."

"Give Odessa a call," Nick suggested. "Her cousin Jimmy is a realtor. He can help you find something."

"Good idea," she smiled. "I was going to check out some areas over the next few days to see what appeals to me. There are some open houses tomorrow I might stop by, too."

As they debated the pros and cons of different neighbourhoods, they missed a dark sedan slowly driving by. The diver, hidden behind the tinted glass, gave them a nasty look. They were getting too close to finding the truth.

***

After meeting with Elizabeth Northam, Tyler felt like he was very close to finally getting a break. He couldn't quite pinpoint what that break would be, but he was sure that he was close.

Tyler looked over the information Ava and Nick uncovered about Studio 416 and the man known as Antonio DiPalma. Sharon and DiPalma knew each other. They indeed appeared very friendly in the pictures. Was he the mysterious man Sharon's ex thought she was seeing? Did he have something to do with Sharon's death? How did he end up in the Halifax harbour so far from here?

Tyler made several inquiries with the Royal Canadian Mounted Police, Canada's national police service, regarding

DiPalma/Lowell, Gallery 416 and anything related to its operations and personnel. The RCMP had more extensive resources and specialized in investigating financial crimes as well as any criminal activity related to national security.

Initially, he assumed the key found with Sharon's remains belonged to her, and whoever dumped her body simply missed it. But searches for lockers and safety deposit boxes in Sharon's name or a combination of anyone in her family came up with nothing. Ava later confirmed his suspicion that the key wasn't Sharon's.

Tyler searched again using the names Antonio DiPalma and Anthony Lowell. He cast a Canada-wide net, but so far, there were no hits. He suspected there was more to this story than they were led to believe, and Sharon Novak was at the centre of it. He was pacing in his office when the call he's been waiting for finally came.

"Bonjour, Detective Burnett," the voice on the other end said. "My name is Camille Pasteur, and I'm calling from Revenu Québec. I think I have something you are looking for."

Whatever break he was hoping for, a call from the provincial revenue ministry wasn't something he expected. But as the saying went, he wasn't going to look a gifted horse in the mouth.

"You have me at a disadvantage," he said.

"We have a safety deposit box in our possession that matches the name you were searching for," she paused. "Antonio DiPalma."

"Are you sure?" Tyler asked as his heart pounded with excitement. He didn't expect to get a hit on the name when he entered it into the database.

"Absolutely," she confirmed.

"I'm not going to lie," he told her. "But I never expected to hear from your organization. How did the contents of this safety deposit box end up with your province's revenue agency?"

"It's not as uncommon as you think, Detective," she said. "There are literally hundreds of safety deposit boxes that go unclaimed in our province every year. What do you think happens to these safety deposit boxes when the banks can't find the owners?"

"They send them to you?" Tyler guessed.

"Well, we try to look up the owners, but sometimes, especially when they are out of province or dead, it's hard to track them down," Camille told him. "We do have an online registry where we list names and last known addresses of the owners, but sometimes even that doesn't always guarantee that we find these people. You'd have to know who you were looking for. It's not like you can pick a name and then call us to claim ownership."

"I take it that if someone has a safety deposit box and they keep it a secret from their family, that family won't know to come and look for it."

"Precisely," she confirmed. "You'd be surprised how many people forget that they even have a safety deposit box. It's strange, but it happens."

"You learn something new every day," he said. "Tell me, what types of things do you find in these safety deposit boxes?"

Camille laughed. It was a hearty laugh that he didn't expect.

"Oh, you'd be surprised," she said. "We find anything from love letters, heirlooms, and jewellery to cash and collectables. Occasionally, we even find gold."

"No kidding," he said. "Is that what's in DiPalma's box?"

There was a slow pause on the other end.

"Not exactly," Camille said. "There are several documents that might mean something to you and another smaller box. However, it is missing a key. It looked important, so we didn't try to open it."

"I think that I might have something here that can," Tyler said as he reached for the evidence bag with the key found with Sharon's body. Could the box be what the key opened?

"Okay, then," she said. "Let's talk about how we can get all of this to you."

They made arrangements that covered the necessary requirements on both ends. By the time the conversation ended, Tyler was sure he was one step closer to finding out who killed Sharon.

As Camille made arrangements to courier the contents to Toronto, Tyler sat back at his computer. There were several more leads to follow up on, but he was getting closer.

CHAPTER 17

It was one of those gorgeous Saturdays that were made for a wedding. Nick flicked off the tiny specs of fluff off his shoulder as he inspected his reflection in the mirror. He spent the morning getting ready, fussing with his hair. The black suit fit him like a glove. Although he preferred his jeans and t-shirts, he didn't mind dressing up, especially when he had a hot date lined up.

He sprayed on some cologne and glanced at his watch. If he left now, he'd have enough time to pick up Diana and get to the reception at a reasonable time. With one last look in the mirror, he went downstairs, grabbed his keys, wallet and phone. He texted Diana to let her know he was on his way.

Outside he bumped into Ava.

"Oh, hey," she said as she looked him up and down. "You clean up nice."

"You gotta stop giving me all these compliments," Nick flashed her one of his smiles. "It's all gonna go to my head."

"As if your head could get any bigger," she laughed. "This is your cousin's wedding? I can't remember."

"My friend, John's," he reminded her. "I have a date with his cousin Diana."

"Well, you kids have fun," Ava said as he started to walk away. "I'm going to check out some open houses."

"Don't forget the panic button," Nick called out to her as he got into his car.

"Yeah, yeah, yeah."

Ava waved as he drove off. Since her parents had tickets to the opera that evening and Stan was busy with his friend across the street, maybe it was time for her to find herself a hot date. With that in mind, she went inside and grabbed her purse. First, she has some properties to see.

After hitting some open houses, Ava decided that maybe getting a house wasn't what she wanted. Too much maintenance and a lot of space for one person. Perhaps she should look into lofts and condominiums instead? There was a lot to think about. She texted Odessa's cousin Jimmy and set up a meeting with him later in the week. All she had to come up with was a list of what she was looking for and a budget she was comfortable spending. Easy enough, she thought.

Ava decided to head downtown. It's been a while since she visited the waterfront and just enjoyed the city. She jumped on the subway and headed west to Yonge and Bloor. There she changed trains and headed south.

She got off at Union Station and made her way up to street level. During the week, this place was filled with people rushing to and from work to catch their commuter trains home. There were tourists with cameras, suitcases and maps walking around, trying to find their way around.

On game nights, this whole area was filled with sports fans sporting jerseys of whatever home team was playing that day. It was all so typical. So ordinary.

Ava headed down Front Street past the cab drivers lined up waiting for fares and just kept walking. Nobody paid any attention to her as they walked by, engrossed in their own lives.

There was something comforting about the anonymity the city provided. Here, at this moment, she wasn't Sharon Novak's daughter to be pitied or whispered about. She was just an ordinary woman walking around downtown.

It was another beautiful day in the city. The warm days of summer still lingered, but the humidity was gone. Ava made her way, passing the CN Tower, Toronto's signature icon standing above the city like a blade. It made her smile, just like it did every time she saw it. Whether Ava wanted to admit it or not, Toronto was her home. It's always been home, no matter where she lived. That's probably why she made the decision to get a place here.

The waterfront was busy as usual as people flocked to the water. The city created a little beach here filled with umbrellas that attracted young and old. Ava made her way past the busy bike lanes along Queens Quey and headed for the park overlooking Lake Ontario. She opted to sit on a bench under the tree. It gave her a great view of the beach and the Toronto Islands across the water.

She got her phone out and opened the dating app Lori told her to try. She downloaded it a few days ago but didn't yet have a chance to set it up. No better time like the present. It's been a while since she tried online dating. Ava forgot how many questions they asked. After spending a lot longer than she intended answering personal questions, she gave up.

Ava got up from the bench. Maybe walking would help her think. The boardwalk along the Harbourfront was still busy. She navigated between couples, children and joggers, trying to decide whether she should grab some dinner or head back home.

"Ava," the sound of a familiar voice made her turn around.

"Oh, hey," she smiled.

***

"Gorgeous evening," Kevin said as he gave her a quick hug. "What are you doing in this area?"

"Oh, you know, just enjoying the evening," she told him. "I've been looking at open houses all day, and I'm exhausted."

"Are you thinking of buying a house then?"

"I'm thinking about it," she said. "My grandfather is thinking of selling the house, so I will need a place of my own."

"Oh yeah," he nodded. "Having your own palace is very freeing. Are you heading back, or do you maybe want to grab a drink?

Ava thought about it for a moment. She didn't have that many friends in town, and with Nick and Odessa at the wedding, she didn't have anyone else to hang out with.

"Sure," she smiled at him. "As long as I'm not intruding on your plans."

"Oh, not at all," he shrugged. "This is a little embarrassing. I was supposed to meet this girl for a drink, but she never showed up."

"Oh, that's terrible," Ava said sympathetically. "Maybe she's just running late?"

"Nah," Kevin said as he shoved his hands in his pockets. "We were supposed to meet an hour ago. When she didn't show, I texted her, and she blew me off."

"Ouch," Ava said. "I've been hesitating to sign up for those online dating apps again. The last time I did, it wasn't great."

"You just wait till I tell you some of the stories," he smiled at her. "Let's get some drinks first."

They chose a bar with a patio that overlooked the water. They talked about simple things. The weather, books, latest movies and shows they liked. It reminded Ava that there was more to life than living in the past. Kevin did indeed entertain her with some wild stories and dates from hell. She realized that she was having more fun than she expected.

"So tell me," he said as they split an order of nachos. "Why the apps? I would have thought someone like you would have guys all over her all the time."

"Come now," she laughed. "I'm not exactly great at relationships. A lot of guys get put off by what I do."

"They do? Well, their loss then," he said between bites. "I think what you do is fascinating."

"Well, you might be a bit biased," she teased. "But my work is not always conducive to healthy relationships."

She felt a bit weird and excused herself to the bathroom. She must have had too much cheese, Ava thought. It always did a number on her stomach. In the bathroom, she felt a bit queasy. Nausea came on fast, and it was ugly.

After she threw up, Ava splashed some water on her face and felt a little bit better.

"Everything okay?" Kevin asked when she got back to the table.

"Yes, I just need some water," after several sips, she felt her stomach settle a bit. She was done with the nachos.

"I saw online that you've made some progress with Sharon's case?"

"Yes and no," she said. "Sharon kept copies of documents that we think prove there was something illegal going on at the place she worked. We put the information out there to see if it generates some leads."

"Oh? What did you uncover?"

"There was definitely something shady going on at the gallery," she thought about it for a moment. "Maybe it would make sense to do another meetup? Just about Sharon's case."

"You want to do a meetup?"

"Yes, I think showing people what we have and what was really going on there would help clear Sharon and bring her killer to justice."

"Are you okay?" he asked.

"Huh?" Suddenly everything started to look a bit fuzzy, and she began to feel dizzy. "I don't feel good."

"Let me give you a ride," Kevin got up and put his arm around her, then guided her out of the bar. He was strong. A lot stronger than she anticipated. Something wasn't right. Ava's head started spinning even more then everything went black.

"I'm sorry it had to come to this," he said as he pushed her into the trunk of his car and shut it.

Something was definitely wrong, Ava thought. She couldn't keep her eyes open. Kevin. He did something to her. With her strength fading, Ava tried to reach the panic button she fastened to her necklace. She could barely move her fingers. How many times was she supposed to tap it? She tapped it with all the willpower she had left as she slipped into unconsciousness.

***

The wedding was in full swing. Nick went through the motions without feeling a lot of enthusiasm. The speeches, the toasts, the cake cutting, the dancing. There were a couple hundred guests in attendance, and he knew most of them. Yet, he was bored.

Steve sat down beside him and set his glass on the table.

"Why aren't you out on the dance floor?" he asked. "Diana is looking mighty good these days."

Nick looked over at his date. She looked stunning in her sleek backless dress, her hair trailing down her bare back in fancy curls. They got their own party started when he went to pick her up, and there was a lot more where that came from. Diana was a looker, and in theory, she was perfect. Yet, she bored him to death.

"She always looks great," Nick said. "In and out of the clothes."

"So why aren't you over there with her right now?" Steve laughed as he slapped Nick's back. "What happened to easy and uncomplicated?"

"Nothing happened," Nick told him. "Been there, done that."

"Bro, you don't know what the hell you want," Steve shook his head in disbelief. "Want another drink?"

"Can't. I'm driving."

"Sucks to be you," he laughed. "Take that stick out of your ass and come on the dance floor. The girls are waving at us."

Nick got up and followed his cousin on the dance floor. Odessa and Diana were already there, surrounded by their friends. The music was loud, and the crowd made it even louder. He should've gotten a ride. At least then, he would have been able to drink.

"Hey you," Diana skillfully wrapped herself around him. Her tongue trailed along his neck up to his ear. She described several colourful suggestions for their own afterparty as someone accidentally bumped into them.

"Nick," Odessa gave him a big smile. "You finally came on the dance floor."

Nick smiled at her as Diana's grip on him loosened. "I did."

"I put Ava in touch with my cousin Jimmy," she yelled into his ear. "I'm sure he'll be able to help her find something."

"I'm sure he will."

Odessa danced to the music as several other women joined in. Diana joined them in singing as well.

"Are you still going to work for her?" Odessa asked.

"What?"

"Ava," she yelled again. "Are you going to keep working for her?"

"I don't know," Nick yelled back. The truth was he didn't know what was going to happen. Their arrangement was temporary. Would she want him around? Better yet, would he want to keep working for her? It wasn't something he was going to wonder about right now.

The music switched to a slow number, and the dance floor filled with couples. He pulled Diana closer to him as she put her arms around his neck. He wrapped his arms around her waist as they swayed to the music.

"You know," she said. "We could get out of here and go back to my place. Finish up what we started."

"We could," he said. Maybe that would take his mind off things. "I don't have anywhere to be tomorrow."

"Hmmm," she lifted her mouth to his and kissed him slowly. "Neither do I."

She slid her arms down his chest and under his jacket. "Is this your phone vibrating?"

Nick reached inside in his jacket pocket. He left it unbuttoned and forgot the phone was there. When he looked at the screen, his heart skipped a beat. It was an alert activated by Ava's panic button. It came in almost an hour ago.

"Shit," he said. "I'll be right back."

Nick ran out to the hallway, trying to call Ava on his way. There was no answer. He tried again.

"Steve," he called out to his cousin, who was getting a drink from the bar. "I have to go. It's an emergency. Can you make sure Diana gets home okay?"

"Sure," Steve said. "What's happened?"

"It's Ava," Nick told him. "I think she's in trouble."

As he ran to his car, Nick called Detective Burnett.

***

Ava drifted in and out of consciousness. Dizzy and confused, she tried to move, but every attempt to open her eyes sent her back into oblivion. She could hear voices, familiar ones that sounded as if she was hearing them underwater. Everything hurt, but she couldn't move. Couldn't make the pain go away.

She tried to speak, but it came out more like a groan. An incoherent sound that couldn't possibly be her. Was it? Why couldn't she move?

"Wake up, sleepyhead," the voice said.

Someone brushed the hair from her face as she tried to open her eyes again. Slowly the face swam into focus.

"Kevin?" Ava blinked. "What did you do to me? Where am I?"

She couldn't move. Ava realized she was sitting in a chair, her arms tied together with a rope. Another rope tied her to the back of the chair. Her feet were bound and tied to the chair's back legs, making it impossible to move.

She tried to move her arms, but it only made the rope dig tighter into her skin. She tried to look around to figure out where they were. It was dark and dingy, like a warehouse that hasn't been used in a while.

"Kevin, what did you do?" she asked.

"What did I DO?" he asked, his eyes bulging freakishly as he stared at her. "It's not what I did. It's what YOU did."

"Kevin," she repeated his name. "Whatever you think I did, I'm sure we can talk about it."

"NO," he started pacing in front of her. "You should have let it go. But, no. You're just like her. You were going to ruin everything."

"Kevin," she tried again.

"Shut up," he growled, the back of his hand cracked loudly across her face.

The pain was so unexpected and made her eyes water. She blinked the tears away, not wanting to give him the satisfaction of seeing her cry, but he wasn't looking at her. He absently rubbed his knuckle, the one that split her lip open, and continued to pace, muttering to himself.

The whole situation felt like some weird nightmare she couldn't get out of. Why would Kevin kidnap her, and why was he so mad at her? Ava wanted to ask more questions but couldn't tell if that would piss him off even more. She definitely didn't want to antagonize him.

Stay calm, she told herself and tried to get a better sense of her surroundings.

The building had solid, concrete walls and a dirty floor. She was in what could have at some point been a hallway with dark, empty doorways gaping on either side. There were no windows, the only light shining from a space above her. It wasn't even a window, but a gap in the floor that let in enough light from somewhere she couldn't see.

Ava could make out a wall in the distance. If there was a door, it was likely behind her. There were no sounds of traffic, no birds chirping, no voices. Where did he take her?

"Kevin, why am I here?"

He didn't respond. She watched him pace as she tried to loosen the rope around her wrists. Her body felt stiff and sore, but she wasn't giving up. Ava had no idea how long she's been there, but surely someone would be looking for her. She remembered her panic button. Did she press it? Ava couldn't remember.

As far as she could tell, the button was still on the chain. She could feel it under her shirt. Ava hoped the pressure from the rope was enough to create pressure that could imitate someone pressing on it.

Kevin continued to pace, muttering to himself. He seemed agitated and out of sorts. It was so unlike him. The Kevin she knew was shy, funny and kind. Not at all like the man she was looking at right now. He must have slipped her something in the food or in her drink. Maybe that's why she puked.

"What the hell are you doing?" he stopped in front and jerked the rope around her wrists.

"The ropes are so tight," she said, trying for sympathy. "They are hurting me. Can't you loosen them up?"

"Do you think I'm stupid or something?" he barked. "That I'm gonna fall for your tricks?"

"No, of course, not," she said calmly, lifting her bound wrists to demonstrate. "But I am in pain. It really hurts."

He stared at her as if considering her words.

"Please, Kevin. You're hurting me," she tried again.

He reached over and yanked her wrist again. She tried not to flinch as he brought his face to hers, those crazy eyes staring into hers. Suddenly, a big smile spread across his face, reminding her of the Kevin she thought she knew. However, that small glimmer of hope was short-lived as he yanked her bound hands, then let them drop back into her lap.

"Nice try," the smile was now cruel, just like his eyes. "I'm not falling for your tricks."

"I'm not…" whatever she was going to say was cut off by another vicious backhanded slap across the face that knocked her and the chair to the floor. Her head hit something hard, and everything went dark.

CHAPTER 18

Tyler wasn't quite ready to pack it up and go home. The reports from RCMP should be arriving at any moment, and he was still waiting for the delivery from Quebec. He could put in a couple more hours as he waited.

His stomach growled, reminding him that he hasn't eaten in a while. He looked down at the coffee cup on his desk. The coffee got cold hours ago, but he didn't have time to get another. As he searched his desk for any spare granola bars, there was a knock on his door.

"Hey Tyler," Duncan, the officer on duty at the front desk, poked his head in. "You got a package."

Duncan was recovering from a minor surgery that temporarily forced him off the streets, but he took it in stride. Some days Tyler suspected that he actually enjoyed working the desk. Maybe he even missed his calling as a mailman.

"Thanks," Tyler said as he got the large box from Duncan and set it on his desk. It was bigger than he imagined, but then again, what did he know about the size of a safety deposit box.

Once he started to open it, he realized the actual content was packed in a larger container to preserve it.

Camille included a note listing all the official content. He gleaned through it then put it aside. He wanted to know what else was in there.

Tyler flipped through the papers. They were receipts for commissioned works. Some included descriptions of the artwork in question, fees and the client's name. He put the papers aside and reached for the locked box.

It was metal, maybe the size of a shoebox with no markings of any kind. On top was a keyhole that he assumed unlocked the box. He put the box down and grabbed the evidence bag with the key found with Sharon's remains.

"Well, here comes nothing."

He placed the key in the hole and turned. Something clicked, and the box unlocked. Tyler sighed with relief and lifted the lid. Finally, he was getting his hands on some answers.

Inside the box were three bound books. After flipping through them, Tyler recognized that they were detailed ledgers. Neatly organized by date, name and the corresponding fees. He picked up the receipts and made a quick comparison. They would have to do a more detailed analysis, but it jived with what he suspected so far. Two sets of books.

After flipping through some pages, Tyler noticed that some accounts had additional notes neatly written beside them.

They weren't just for the artwork. He recognized the names, but that didn't make sense. He checked the commissioned art made by DiPalma. Something wasn't right here. Antonio DiPalma did a lot more than just produce mediocre art. He created forgeries.

Tyler sat down in his chair and stared at what he found. Was this enough to kill Sharon over? DiPalma was closely tied with the gallery, and that connected him to Adam Walker. The chances of Adam not knowing what DiPalma was up to were slim. They must have been in on it together.

Straight as an arrow, that's how Stan described Sharon. Perhaps she really was. Tyler played it out in his head. Sharon found out what they were up to, confronted them about it. Maybe they tried to pay her off at first, but she didn't go for it. She didn't give up, perhaps even threatened to expose the scheme, and one of them killed her when she wouldn't budge.

Was that why Adam was so afraid of her even now? She threatened to expose him. He would have lost everything, including his chances at a political career. Then why not just say that when Tyler asked him about it?

There were more things in the metal box. He put the books aside and looked inside, and pulled out a small, leather wallet. Inside was Sharon's driver's license, a couple of credit cards and a few other documents.

Did DiPalma kill Sharon and hide her body? Tyler didn't peg Walker as someone who liked to get his hands dirty. As he was about to take out the envelope from the bottom of the box, his phone rang.

"Burnett," he answered and listened as Nick filled him in. "Come straight to the station."

***

When Ava came to, she was lying on the floor, still tied to the chair. Her head was pounding, her neck sore. At least she was still alive, and that had to count for something. She kept her eyes closed as she tried to understand what was going on around her. She could hear a muffled voice—she assumed it was Kevin's and not much else.

Ava had no idea how long she's been out or how long it's been since she had drinks with Kevin on the patio. Something was caked to her face, and she realized it was likely dried blood. She counted herself lucky since the blow to her head could have easily killed her. Ava thought of Stan and how pale he looked lying there in a hospital. She wondered if anyone would ever find her.

"I said I had it under control," Kevin's voice interrupted her thoughts. "Stop telling me what to do."

He paced around some more and walked over to where Ava lay on the floor. He nudged her with his foot, and when she didn't immediately respond, he kicked harder. Her eyes widened, and she gasped in pain.

"She's fine," he said to whoever was on the other side of the phone. "I told you, I got this."

Kevin ended the call and slipped the phone into his back pocket. He dragged her by the hair until the chair was in the upright position again. He flipped a bucket upside down and sat on it access from her.

"It's time we had a little chat," he told her.

"Why am I here?" she asked.

"You're here because I said so," he spat out.

"What do you want? Money?"

He only snorted in disgust.

"Oh please, don't insult me," he said. "You're here because you fucked up. You will be punished for what you did. "

She wondered about the countless women she covered in her stories. Those that disappeared and those that were eventually found dead. How many of them faced situations like this? How many of them lived to tell the tale? Not many. She didn't want to be one of them.

"What do you think I did, Kevin?" she asked.

She had no idea how much time had passed since he took her. It must have been hours ago. That surely would be enough time for her family to notice her missing. What about the alert? Did it go through like it was supposed to? Unless someone found her soon, she was on her own. She needed to keep Kevin talking.

Ava didn't even know where she was. If he took her somewhere out of town, chances of someone finding her were slim. Were they near Mitchell's house? Where the black pickup truck tried to run them off the road?

"Tell me what I did," she demanded. "How am I supposed to know what I did if you won't tell me?"

Kevin looked at her as if the thought hadn't occurred to him.

"You ruined my family," he said, his face dangerously close to hers. "You destroyed everything, Sharon."

Ava blinked. Wait, what? Why would Kevin think she was Sharon? This didn't make any sense.

"Kevin," she said quietly. "I'm Ava. You know me. I have a podcast that you listen to. You are my friend."

"SHUT UP," he yelled and got in her face. This time she flinched, bracing for another blow. Instead, he got up to his feet and rubbed his face with his hands. "I'm so tired of you constantly deflecting things. Just tell me where it is."

"Where is what?"

"Sharon made up lies about my family," he said, and Ava hoped he wasn't confusing them right now. "Lies that would have ruined us. She destroyed everything and recorded everything to make sure it happened. I want it back."

When she just stared at him, he lashed out, "Where is it?"

"I don't have it," she said. "I'm sorry, I don't have anything. Sharon didn't leave anything."

"Liar," another slap had her seeing stars. "Sharon destroyed my family. You said you had her things. You were going to expose them online. The same thing she threatened to expose. Lies, it was all lies, but she didn't care who she hurt. You are just like her."

Nothing about this made sense. Who was his family? The Northams? Ava could feel the sting from the blows, the pain shooting up her arms and legs from the binds. Her back was numb, and her neck ached like the devil.

She had to keep him talking.

"I'm so sorry about your family," Ava told him. "I'm sorry that you believe Sharon tried to hurt them. But I don't think that's true."

"Don't lie to me," he yelled. "I know the truth. She told me the truth."

***

Stan, Michael and Joan sat around a table in one of the station's meeting rooms. Nick opted to lean against the wall. Tyler set up the family there as the frantic search for Ava continued. There was coffee on the table, but nobody was drinking it. They all dealt with the situation in various stages of grief and panic.

Joan and Michael sat together, holding hands. You could tell they both have cried at one point or another. Ava's alert didn't get to them in time as Michael had his phone turned off during the performance. Now he was stricken with guilt for watching the opera while someone took his baby. Stan, still not fully recovered from his accident, alternated between pacing and sitting down. For him, the situation was eerily too familiar.

Nick looked up as Tyler walked in with another man.

"This is Detective Jones," he told the family. "He's the lead detective in charge of this investigation."

Detective Marcus Jones was a tall, dark-skinned man with the flat eyes of a cop that has seen more than the average person. He had a commanding presence without saying a word. He scanned the room, getting a feel for the players.

"You have something?" Nick asked.

"We're working with the monitoring service to locate the device," Jones said. "The system logs where the original alert came from. Once activated, it can be tracked. We're also working with the phone company to try to trace her phone. If she still has it on her, we'll be able to get a location."

"Do you have any ideas as to who could have taken her?" Michael asked.

"Not yet," Jones looked at Burnett and moved over to give him room. "But we might have a lead."

Tyler laid out evidence bags with the items from the safety deposit box on the table. There was a small gasp when he put down the wallet.

"Is that what I think it is?" Stan asked as he looked up from the wallet to Tyler. "You found Sharon's wallet?"

"Can you positively identify it as hers?" Tyler asked.

"Yes. My wife and I bought it for her," he said. "I would know it anywhere."

"Where did you find it?" Michael asked again.

Tyler watched them process the news. Stan sat down, his eyes filling with tears.

"There was a small key found with Sharon's remains," Tyler explained. "We still probably wouldn't have known what it opened if someone didn't break into Mr. Novak's house."

"Did Sharon's killer break into my house?" Stan asked.

"Not exactly," Tyler said. "The DNA we collected at your house matched a sample taken from a man found in Halifax harbour in 2009. When his body was found, he had a fake ID on him with the name Anthony Lowell. They figured out that the ID was fake, but they had no other leads."

"Antonio DiPalma," Nick said. "He's the man who worked at the gallery."

"I know that name," Stan said suddenly. "He was an artist. Sharon brought him around once or twice. He seemed like a nice man. Are you saying that he killed my daughter?"

"We are not sure, but that's a possibility," Tyler said. "After I got his name, I searched again and got a hit on an old safety deposit box in Quebec. All these items, including Sharon's wallet, were inside."

"There is no mention of him in the original investigation," Nick said. "Wouldn't they interview him after Sharon went missing? He was connected to the gallery."

"Unfortunately, over time, records got lost or were misplaced," Tyler told him. "Since the original investigator can't be questioned about it, I don't have the answers for that."

"What about when they found him?" Joan chimed in. "Why didn't they put it together?"

"Well,," Tyler said. "Back in 2009, technology wasn't what it is today. Nobody reported DiPalma missing, so he wasn't in any databases as a missing person. Unfortunately, there are backlogs as well. Information between provinces gets lost, or it takes time before it ends up in the right hands."

"So if he's not the one who broke into my house," Stan said. "Then who was it?"

"We think that person is his son."

Jones looked down at his phone as it buzzed. He read the message then looked up at them.

"I think we got something," he said. "Excuse me, I need to check on this."

***

"Who told you the truth?" Ava asked. "Why do you think Sharon's things will ruin your family?"

"I'm the one asking questions," he said as he grabbed her throat with his hand, tightening the grip around it. "Where did you hide Sharon's things?"

"Everything is at home," she managed as his hand loosened slightly. "Everything is at home in my office. I can take you there."

Teeth bared, he looked at her in disgust.

"I told you not to lie to me," he said, his grip tightening. "I already checked your house. It wasn't there."

The realization came down on her like a pile of bricks. Kevin, the guy she trusted all this time, was the one that broke in and hurt her grandfather. He was the one that broke into the house and put Stan in the hospital. Ava recalled all the times she ran into him in the neighbourhood and wondered if those run-ins weren't random at all.

"I know who you are," she said. "You're DiPalma's son. The man who has his art featured at the gallery where Sharon worked."

"Very good. Now you're getting it," he said. She prepared herself for another blow, but it never came. "My father was a visionary. A prolific artist ahead of his time. He had his works displayed in galleries all over the world. Not just here at Studio 416."

As Kevin got lost in his memories, Ave was doing her best to loosen the ropes. She had to keep him busy and talking.

"My father was a man with a vision," he continued. "Sharon didn't appreciate his talents."

"Did your father kill Sharon?" she asked.

"Your mother destroyed him," he said with disgust. "She destroyed his career."

"How?" she asked. "Tell me how you think she destroyed his career."

He looked like he was considering the words, trying to make sense of things in his head. If she could put doubt in his mind, maybe he'd let her go.

"Stop talking," he said. "You're trying to confuse me with your lies.

"I'm not lying," she said. "Think about it. Your father died in a car accident in Halifax years later. Sharon had nothing to do with his death."

"No, no, no," he muttered. "You're just like her. Always lying and trying to manipulate me."

"I'm not," she said in her defence. "I'm not lying, and I'm not trying to manipulate you."

"Shut up," his fist slammed into her face. She could feel the pain as her vision blurred.

Before Ava got a chance to say anything, Kevin's phone rang. He looked at the screen then back at her before he answered it.

"What?" he snarled at the caller as he walked away.

She couldn't make out what he was saying, but Ava could tell he was angry even from where she was sitting. At this point, it didn't matter whether he was mad at her or at the caller. She just hoped he would stop hitting her.

The pain was excruciating, but she couldn't give up. She tried to stretch her neck and force her muscles to contract in short spurts to keep the circulation going. Ava wiggled her toes and fingers while trying to look around for something that could function as a weapon. She needed to loosen up the ropes if she wanted to get out of here.

Ava didn't hear him approach. He walked up behind, grabbed her hair and tugged her head back. She gasped in shock and from the pain.

"I told you," he said close to her ear. "No funny business."

"I wasn't doing anything," she told him.

"Women like you are always scheming," he muttered as he let go of her hair. "Always lying."

"I'm not," she told him. "I want to help you."

For several moments he just stood there staring at her. She could see glimpses of the Kevin she thought she knew, but Ava realized that Kevin never existed. The man standing before was a stranger. A violent, unpredictable man who wasn't afraid to use violence to get what he wanted.

Those cold, dead eyes stared at her mockingly. His mouth twisted in a grim smile. His hand closed around her neck as he whispered menacingly, "Don't try anything stupid. I have to get something, and then I'll deal with you."

Ava covered hundreds of cases of missing people. Many of them were abducted and killed. There was always a sense of dread and sadness when dealing with stories like that. Still, she never expected to go through something like this herself. She had no doubt that whatever he was getting, it wouldn't end well for her. He was going to kill her.

Ava thought of Stan. Her grandfather was always there for her, cheering her on. Pushing his own pain aside to aid her quest for Sharon. Her death would surely kill him. Of that, she had no doubt. Just thinking about it brought her to tears.

Her parents? Well, they would be crushed too, but at least they had each other. That fact didn't make it easier, but it gave her some comfort. Ava never cleared things up with her father after what Joan told her. She never told him she loved him and understood why he never told her the truth about Joan.

Joan, the caring, supportive and loving mother that's always been there for her. The woman who made her realize that she wasn't like Sharon. Ava always used her parent's failed marriage as an excuse for why she wasn't good with relationships. Joan made her realize that she was wrong.

Ava didn't want to live with regrets. Didn't want to become another missing woman who ended up dead at the hands of a madman. She jerked her legs in frustration and realized that the rope binding them to the chair came loose. She stretched her legs in front of her and groaned at the sensation. There was hope yet.

CHAPTER 19

As Jones went to check on the investigation, Tyler laid out the rest of the items. There were pictures, documents and notebooks.

"What's this?" Nick asked as he looked down at the pictures. Something clicked as he picked a small photo in the evidence bag. "Is this what I think it is?"

Michael and Joan moved closer for a better look as well.

"What is it?" Stan asked.

"These documents and pictures identify Kevin DiPalma as Antonio DiPalma's son," Tyler said. "He's been going by Smith, which is the reason he was never flagged."

"Do you think he's the one that took Ava?" Nick asked. Small things started to fall into place. "He was very interested in Sharon's case. I'm sure he would have seen the pictures and information we posted online. Ava wouldn't have been suspicious of him."

"It's possible," Tyler said. "Jones is running his name as we speak. We're trying to locate him, but nothing so far. He's not in his residence."

"What does this all have to do with Sharon?" Stan asked. "Did this DiPalma kill my daughter? And is his son now the one who took Ava? For what purpose?"

"We're still trying to put all the pieces together," Tyler assured him. "Unfortunately, we think there is more."

"What do you mean?"

"We suspect Kevin is also responsible for the death of Adam Walker and Frank Mitchell, the original investigator on Sharons' case."

"Let me get this straight," Michael said with an edge in his voice. "You're telling me that that man who killed two people, if not more, is the same man who took my daughter?"

"Mr. Reed," Tyler told him calmly. "We are doing everything we can to find your daughter. We will find her."

"This is Sharon all over," he said as he sank into his chair and looked over at Stan. Joan dabbed nervously at her eyes with a tissue.

"No, Michael," Stan shook his head. "This is not like Sharon. We know who took Ava. We know who the murderous son of a bitch is, and we're going to get her back."

"Why would Kevin kill Adam Walker?" Nick asked.

"I don't have an answer for that yet," Tyler told him. "But I know we're getting close."

"Could Adam have anything to do with that man's death? Kevin's father?" Michael asked. He was sitting down again, tapping his fingers nervously on the table.

"It's unlikely. DiPalma's death was deemed an accident," Tyler said. "Dangerous roads, bad weather. A driver not familiar with road hazards loses control of the car and ends up in the water. It happens more often than you think."

"What does this all have to do with Sharon and the documents she hid?" Stan asked. "You said before that they were records. What do these two men have to do with those records?"

"We think something was going on at the gallery that wasn't exactly legal. The accounts Sharon documented point to off-shore accounts for multiple shell corporations," Tyler said. "According to the RCMP records, they had the gallery under surveillance. I'm still trying to get more information on what they were investigating."

"When this all went down, Kevin was just a kid," Nick said. "Why would it matter to him now if his father, who's been out of his life for years, was connected to Sharon's death? Nobody knows their connection, so why bring it up?"

"I don't think it's his father's connection that prompted it all," Tyler said as he picked up one of the documents in the clear evidence bags. "It's his mother's."

"Who is his mother?" Michael asked.

"Elizabeth Northam," Tyler said. "She has a lot more at stake if this came out than any of them."

"Are you kidding me?" Nick said in disbelief. "Elizabeth Northam is Kevin's mother? How did we miss that?"

"That's exactly what I asked myself," Tyler said. "Why would a mother hide the existence of a child? Nothing in her records states that she has one."

"According to this birth certificate," Nick said as he looked at it. "Kevin was born in Vancouver. That's far from home."

"The way it's playing out for us is that Elizabeth's father didn't approve of the relationship," Tyler explained. "DiPalma was an artist and not exactly a good one. Based on what I've found about him, Northam wouldn't allow his daughter to get involved with someone like that. They were never married. At least there are no records of marriage anywhere. Maybe that was to hide the relationship from her father."

"That would explain why she flew across the country to give birth."

"More than that," Tyler handed him several other documents. "Looks like Kevin was raised by DiPalma's side of the family at least till George Northam died."

***

As soon as Kevin left, Ava increased her efforts of getting freed from the ropes. She didn't have any time to waste. When Kevin came back, that could be the end for her. He made it clear that he wasn't going to let her go, and she wasn't going to test that theory. If he was going to kill her, she might as well make it as difficult as she could. She was done being a victim. All the anger raging through her gave her strength she didn't know she had.

After some effort, she was able to bring her wrists to her mouth and tried to loosen the rope. By rotating her wrists back and forth, she was able to slacken the rope just enough to maneuver the knot, enough to pull at it with her teeth. The rope wasn't budging at first, but after a few minutes of trying, she could finally wiggle her hands free.

Ava almost cried as she saw the raw skin on her wrists. But there was no time for self-pity. Ignoring the pain, she clenched her hands to get the circulation going again. When the numbness subsided, she started working on the ropes, tying her to the chair. By expanding and contracting her muscles as much as she could, she was able to loosen the rope just enough to make some space between her and the chair.

Her arms were still tied to her body with the rope, and she was still bound to the chair. The rope wasn't that thick, but there was a lot of it. She could loosen the outer rope enough for it to fall, but the other was one tighter. Ava tried to sway back and forth to loosen it as much as she could.

Somewhere in the distance, she heard footsteps approaching. She needed to get out of the binds before Kevin got back. Desperate to get the ropes off her, she whimpered as her arms rubbed against the rope. She was close but wasn't fast enough.

A light suddenly went on. One of those creepy blue lights came from the bulbs sticking out of the walls on either side. She didn't notice them before. Then again, she was a little preoccupied with staying alive.

There was a loud thump as if he dropped something heavy on the floor. Loud footsteps followed. He was on her before she even registered what was happening.

"What the fuck are you doing?" Kevin yelled. He grabbed her by the throat and squeezed so hard she almost blacked out. "I told you not to try anything. Didn't I? But you don't listen. They never fucking listen."

He was going to kill her. She was sure of it. There was no talking him down anymore. His face was red with fury, and his hands tightened around her neck. She didn't come this far to let him win. He didn't notice that the ropes binding her feet came free. He also made the mistake of standing over her, his legs straddling hers.

"Fuck you," she managed as she kicked up her legs with everything she had and kneed him straight in the balls.

Surprise flashed in his eyes as he bent over in pain, loosening the grip on her neck. Not taking any chances, Ava shut her eyes and aimed her forehead into his nose with all the power she could muster. She heard a slight crunch as his blood trickled down his face. She felt a small sense of satisfaction. But this was far from over.

As Kevin groaned on the floor, she managed to free herself and started to remove the rest of the ropes. She still wasn't completely free, but at least she was out of that damn chair. As she fought against the remaining restraints, Ava could finally see the rest of the space where he held her. There was a doorway just down that creepy hallway that could be her ticket out.

She managed to get herself up, but her muscles were so stiff she almost fell on the floor. Ava reached under her shirt until she found the panic button. She pressed it down several times as she tried to move away.

She didn't notice the rope tangled by her feet until Kevin tugged at it. She stumbled and fell on the concrete floor. Pain shot through her as her knee connected with the ground. Kevin, his face filled with rage, managed to bring himself up. He winced as he moved towards her.

Ava desperately tried to claw away, but he was almost on top of her. It was then she saw the pile he dropped on the floor. There was a tarp, more ropes and a shovel. She didn't want to think about what he planned to do with that.

"Let me go," she yelled as she tried to kick at him.

"I told you that you're not going anywhere," he growled. "You broke my fucking nose, you stupid bitch."

She clearly didn't kick him in the balls hard enough. He was bleeding as he grabbed for the rope and reached down to her feet. He was going to tie her up again. She wasn't going to make it easy. As he bent over her feet, she kicked as hard as she could. Those kickboxing lessons were finally paying off.

He swore again, clutching at his nose. Ava managed to get to her feet and grabbed the shovel, ready to smash him with it. At this point, she didn't care if only one of them would be coming out alive. As long as it was her.

"You're going to pay for this," he told her. He was on his knees, holding himself up with one arm while wiping his nose with the other. "I should have killed you when I had the chance. I should have taken care of that assistant of yours too, just like I did the old man. There will be time for that, but for now, I'll settle for you."

"Not today, asshole," she was ready to smash the shovel in his face as he was about to lunge at her. Out of nowhere, two shots rang out somewhere behind her. She ducked, hoping the bullet didn't hit her. It only took seconds to realize it wasn't aimed at her.

Time moved in slow motion. Ava watched the surprise on Kevin's face as he looked down at the small hole in his chest. His hand reached for the spot only to fall away. Blood soaked through his shirt, and he slumped to the floor. Slowly, Ava turned around to face the shooter.

***

Jones came back into the room with a folder and more pictures. He set them down on the table as everyone stared at him with hope.

"It turns out that there are no vehicles registered to Kevin Smith," he told them. "But there are two registered to Kevin DiPalma."

"Let me guess," Nick said. "A dark sedan and a black pickup truck?"

"Bingo," Jones smiled at him. "We also managed to locate Kevin's apartment, and our team is going through it right now. Kevin, as it turns out, was on a lot of powerful medication. He's been hospitalized before and spent some time in a psychiatric facility."

"He seemed so normal," Nick said.

"With the right medication, anyone can lead a functioning and productive life," Jones shrugged. "We won't know all the details about his health until we speak with his doctors. That will take some time."

"You know, I keep thinking that maybe if I paid more attention to him, I could have spotted something sooner," Nick said as he sat down. "If we dug more into his background, maybe we would have found the connection."

"You couldn't have known," Jones told him. "The image he projected was what he wanted everyone to see. An ordinary guy that doesn't stand out. He wanted to be forgettable."

"It was him that followed me, tried to run us off the road," Nick realized. "Was he also the one who set off the dry-ice bomb?"

"We're looking into all of that right now."

Joan walked over to Nick, placed her hand on his shoulder. There was regret and pain in his eyes when he looked at her.

"You got Ava the panic button," she said as she smiled at him warmly. "She used it to alert us that she was in danger. She had that because you gave her that little device."

"I appreciate you saying that," Nick said. "It still doesn't make me feel less guilty."

"She wouldn't want you to feel guilty," Joan told him. "Ava has a good head on her shoulders, but she can be reckless. She wouldn't have gotten the button herself because it wouldn't occur to her. She wouldn't see the need for it. But you did. That alone will save her life."

Nick looked around the table. Stan and Michael nodded in agreement. There was no anger, no blame in their eyes. There was more he could do to find her.

"Detective Jones," he said. "Have you searched for any properties near where the Mitchells live to see if Kevin owns any of them? The car came from that area. He must have a place there somewhere. Maybe that's where he took her."

"We are looking into that," Jones assured him. "Now that we know the connection to Elizabeth Northam, we've expanded our search for properties in her name or anything to do with her company."

"Have you gone to talk to her?" Stan asked. "Maybe she knows something that can tell us where that man took Ava."

"We're unable to locate her at the moment," Jones said. "But we're looking for her as well."

Just then, Nick's phone vibrated, and so did Michael's. They both looked down on the screens just as Tyler rushed back into the room.

"It's the alert," he said. "Looks like Ava activated the panic button again. We're tracing it now."

"Please find my baby," Michael said as he stood up and walked towards Tyler and Jones.

"We'll get her back, Mr. Reed," Jones said as he grabbed his phone. "If he has her stashed somewhere out of town, we'll have to reach out to the locals for assistance. I'll make some calls."

***

"Never leave a man to do a woman's job," the woman said with a smile. "Am I right?"

The gun was now pointed at Ava. The woman strolled towards her, never breaking a smile. She wore dark blue dress pants and a cream blouse under a leather jacket that matched the pants. Her hair was pulled back in a neat bun, not a strand out of place. She seemed perfectly at home, even if she was overdressed for the occasion. When she was close enough, Ava finally recognized her.

Elizabeth Northam glanced down at Kevin's body lying on the floor between them. She kicked him slightly with her boot.

"Is he dead?" she asked.

"I... I don't know," Ava fumbled.

"Well, check," she ordered.

Ava kneeled beside Kevin, slowly setting the shovel down beside her. She checked for a pulse, but there was none. When she looked down, she noticed something poking out of his pants pocket. It looked like a phone.

Ava looked up at Elizabeth and nodded her head in confirmation.

"Well, then," the woman said pleasantly, "It's time for you and me to have a little chat."

With the gun still pointed at Ava, Elizabeth looked around until she spotted the chair. She took several steps towards it. Without taking her eyes off her, Ava reached for the phone in Kevin's pocket. She realized, with some relief, that it was hers.

As Elizabeth grabbed the chair and started dragging it closer, Ava swiped, enabling the camera feature. With a slight glance down, she swiped to video and hit record. She hoped the phone would pick up their conversion in case something happened to her.

Elizabeth brushed her hand across the seat as if dusting it off then sat down. She then motioned with her gun for Ava to sit on the floor beside Kevin.

"Well, then," she crossed her legs and rested her arm on her thigh, the gun aimed at Ava's head. "There is no reason for at least one of us to be comfortable."

"What do you want?" Ava asked.

"Ah, straight to the point," she mused. "I like that."

"Why did you shoot Kevin?"

"So many questions," Elizabeth mused as she looked over at Kevin with distaste. "I'm afraid that Kevin outlived his usefulness. He became a liability, and I can't afford any more mistakes."

Ava's hand inched closer to the shovel but stopped when the woman's eyes bore into hers.

"I wouldn't try that I were you," she warned. "I will put that bullet straight into your brain the moment you try anything funny."

"You're not going to get away with this," Ava said.

"Oh, I can and I will," she smiled coldly. "This is not the first time I've had to clean up a mess."

"What do you want?" Ava asked again.

"That is the question for the ages, isn't it?" she mused. "You have such a bright mind. So much potential. In the right hands, a bright mind can be moulded into a handy tool. You know what the problem is with such clever minds?"

Ava stared at her. "What?"

"They overthink. Ask too many questions. Stick their noses where they don't belong," she curled her lip in distaste. "They have a very short life span. You want something done with no questions asked, you get brawn. They don't get philosophical. They just do the job."

"Which one was Kevin?"

The woman looked amused at the question. She glanced again at Kevin's body lying in a pool of blood.

"Kevin could have been both, but unfortunately for him, he was neither."

Ava looked over at the body as well. She tried to remember the Kevin, who was her friend. The supportive fan who organized meetups for true crime enthusiasts and amateur sleuths. That Kevin likely wasn't real, but it made her feel better to remember him that way.

The body on the floor was a crazy-eyed Kevin who drugged, abducted and beat her. She didn't know who that man was, but the woman holding the gun on her clearly did.

"What does this have to do with me?" Ava asked.

"Oh, it has everything to do with you, my dear," she smiled. "We wouldn't be in this mess if it wasn't for you."

"I don't know what you think I did," Ava said. "But this has to be a mistake. You must be confusing me with someone else."

"I know exactly who you are, Ava Reed," Elizabeth said. The smile was gone now. Her face was cold and ruthless.

CHAPTER 20

"What do you want, Elizabeth," Ava said. She was tired, in pain and seriously dehydrated. She also didn't know how much battery she had left on her phone. Better make this quick.

"Ah, so you do know who I am as well," Elizabeth nodded approvingly. "Not just a pretty face, I see."

"Are you here to pay my compliments, or are you going to tell me what the hell you want?"

Elizabeth laughed. It was a joyful sound that echoed in the empty space, but to Ava, the sound was revolting.

"I think that under different circumstances, I would have enjoyed having you around," Elizabeth said. "You really are a delight."

"What do you want?"

"I want what's mine, of course," Elizabeth shook the gun in Ava's direction. The smile was gone. "What your mother took from me."

"You want Sharon's stuff."

"Sharon stole from us," Elizabeth said impatiently. "My family gave her a job. We took care of her. What did she do to pay us back? She took what didn't belong to her. And now, I want it back."

"And what makes you think that I have it?"

"You know what's been the biggest obstacle in my life?" she asked and continued without waiting for a reply. "I'm surrounded by weak-minded men. They are all so useless. Every single one of them.

"My father was the worst of them. An overbearing buffoon with no respect for female intellect. I expected better from my very own son. But he turned out to be such a disappointment." Elizabeth looked at Kevin's body with distaste.

Ava looked at Kevin, then back at Elizabeth. It finally clicked. How did she miss that?

"You're Kevin's mother," she said. It wasn't a question.

"See? I knew you were bright."

"But you shot him. You killed your own son," Ava said in disbelief.

"Frankly, he was always weak," she tilted her head slightly as if reminiscing about her son's failed potential. "Too emotional. He lacked the brains and the brawn. I had such hopes for him."

The conversation with Burnett came flooding back. The intruder who broke into Stan's house was related to Anthony Lowell. The man they discovered was, in fact, Antonio DiPalma. That means Elizabeth knew DiPalma. She knew Sharon. She thought of the picture of Sharon and DiPalma together.

"What about this father, Antonio DiPalma?" she asked.

"What about him?"

"Was he also a disappointment?"

Elizabeth's head perked up at the question. A smile tugged at the corner of her mouth as she studied Ava. She looked almost amused.

"My, my. Maybe you are smarter than I gave you credit for," she mused. "It seems that you were quite busy digging into the past."

"Must have pissed you off when he got cozy with Sharon, though," Ava said and watched with satisfaction as the smile fell from Elizabeth's face. "Was that what happened? Sharon moved in on your man? That must have pissed you off."

Elizabeth pointed the gun at her and fired. The bullet whizzed by her ear.

"Consider this a warning," she said. "I won't miss the next time."

"While I'd love to chat about your daddy issues," Ava continued. "I already told you that I don't have Sharon's stuff."

"If you're even near as good as your mother was," Elizabeth said. "You have the stuff. Despite being surrounded by many useless men in my life, I chose to surround myself with brilliant women. Sharon was brilliant. I knew that with her at my side, we could have been invincible."

"My mother wasn't a criminal," Ava said flatly.

"There is no need to get hung up on semantics, my dear," Elizabeth's eyes narrowed as they bore into Ava's. "I gave your mother a business opportunity. A chance to make something out of her life using her talents. She was the one who decided she didn't want to play."

"So you decided to eliminate her," Ava said.

"I am always disappointed when a great mind is being wasted," Elizabeth said. "But it's like dealing with a rabid dog. If you can't fix it, you must put it down."

"So you had her killed," Ava said, the realization dawning on her. "Did DiPalma kill my mother?

"I already told you," Elizabeth said flatly. "Never leave a man to do a woman's job." She leaned towards Ava, her eyes filled with distaste. "I killed Sharon. If you don't get me what I want, I'm going to put a bullet between your eyes just like I did to her."

***

"If you're going to kill me anyway," Ava said, "what's my motivation for giving you what you want?"

"This isn't a negotiation, Ava."

"Actually, it is," Ava pointed out. "I have something you want. I'm sure we can come to some sort of an understanding."

"What's stopping me from putting a bullet in your head and then doing the same to your grandfather? Maybe put one in your father's head or that pretty wife of his for good measure?"

"You don't strike me as someone who likes to leave a mess," Ava said. If she was going to die, she wouldn't go down without a fight. "Killing me, my grandfather, my father. That's messy. People are going to ask questions. Besides," she continued. "The police are going to figure this out sooner or later. You see, unlike my mother, I didn't keep the information to myself. I didn't hide it from everyone. The police have copies. I've also uploaded everything to a folder stored in the cloud. There is a trigger date. If I don't recall it, everything Sharon hid will go live."

"You're bluffing."

"Why would I?" Ava asked. "I have resources my mother didn't have. People I can trust. They probably already know who kidnapped me. They are looking for me as we speak. It won't take them long to put things together."

"Is this your idea of a negotiation?" Elizabeth asked. "I'm not scared of the police. They can be bought just as much as anyone else."

It was Ava's turn to smile now. She could see a slight hint of hesitation in Elizabeth's eyes. She was smart, but she didn't know everything.

"Why did you kill Sharon?"

"This is getting tedious now," she stifled a yawn. "Didn't we already cover this?"

"Humour me," Ava said.

"I will not tolerate insolence," Elizabeth's eyes went flat again as she smirked at Ava. She got up and walked up beside Ava. The barrel of her gun firmly pushing into her temple. "Don't fuck with me. If you had what Sharon took, you'd know everything there is to know. You wouldn't be asking me to tell you."

"I'm telling you the truth," Ava said, hoping the cops or somebody got here soon. "I just want to know more about my mother. You knew her. Tell me about her. Please."

Elizabeth considered her words. The gun moved away from her head, but it was still pointed at her.

"Sharon, much like you, was an annoyance. I still don't understand why that idiot Adam hired her. Probably thought she'd sleep with him. So many did in those days," she said with disgust as she started to pace. "He was so taken by her.

Said how brilliant she was. I tried to get my father to talk some sense into him, but he too fell for her charms. Men, always thinking with their dicks." Elizabeth's mouth twisted in distaste. "I told them both that she would ruin everything. And I was right."

"My father always valued his useless illegitimate son over me, his rightful heir. He actually thought his useless idiot would take over the family business. But he couldn't even keep it in his pants long enough to think about business." Elizabeth swore as she kicked a rock and sent it flying across the floor. "He couldn't wait for Adam to take his name when he finally married his mother. But he didn't. I made sure of that."

"What did you do?"

"Blackmail, dear," Elizabeth continued to smirk. "Men are simple creatures. They can be manipulated. My father thought he ran the business, but it was me. I was the one making sure everything went smoothly. And it did. Until Sharon came along."

"She figured it out?"

"Your mother was clever, but it took her a while to put things together," she said. "She got many opportunities to back away, but she just couldn't keep her mouth shut. Tony was supposed to convince her to let it go."

"But she didn't."

"No, she didn't," Elizabeth's mouth turned into a smirk now. "Sharon had great potential. Unfortunately, she wasn't very malleable. She, too, turned out to be such a disappointment."

Straight as an arrow, Stan's words echoed in Ava's mind. Her mother wasn't a criminal mastermind after all. She wanted to do the right thing, and it cost her everything.

"How will I know that once I get you Sharon's stuff, you won't kill me too?" Ava asked.

Elizabeth laughed. "I never said that I wouldn't kill you too."

***

Detective Jones came back with news. They found Ava's location. As Nick suspected, Kevin took her to a property owned by the NorFast group not far from where Mitchell lived.

"We found some evidence that Frank Mitchell was paid off to cover up Sharon's disappearance," he told them. "The RCMP was looking at him for several crimes that went back to when he started on the force."

"I never liked that guy," Stan muttered. "I suspected he knew more than he was saying. Did he even look for Sharon?"

"He was likely paid to look the other way," Tyler said as he walked into the room. "The books Sharon took copies of were payments to different high ranking officials, builders and politicians. The family business paid well, and it bought a lot of loyalty."

"Was Studio 416 even a real gallery?" Nick asked. "That art was nothing spectacular."

"Well, based on what Sharon had, what was in the safety deposit box and what we found at Kevin's apartment, I'd say it was a front."

"A front for what?" Joan asked.

"Anything you can think of," Tyler said as he flipped his folder open and looked through the pages. "Drugs, stolen artifacts, money laundering. It was quite successful for some time before anyone even suspected anything going on."

"So DiPalma wasn't a real artist?" Stan asked.

"He was a different type of an artist," Tyler said. "He was a forger. A very skilled one at that. A trait he tried to pass on to his son."

"Kevin was a forger too?" Nick asked.

"Unfortunately for him, he didn't have his father's talent," Jones chimed in again. "But he was a packrat, and he kept a lot of his father's old stuff. It's like a goldmine of information."

"Does that prove he killed Sharon?" Stan asked. "The father, I mean."

"It doesn't look like it, Mr. Novak."

"How did he end up with her wallet and those other documents?"

"We're still trying to piece that, but he was either cleaning up or took it as evidence."

Another officer poked her head in the door.

"I got the locals on the phone," she said. "They have uniforms on the way. They are sending an ambulance too."

"Patch them through," Jones said. "Let's end this and bring Ava home."

***

"I get where you're coming from, Elizabeth. Your father underestimated you," Ava said as her hand found the hilt of the shovel. "How did you convince him to let you run things?"

"Most men underestimate women," she shrugged. "They walk around like they know everything best. They don't. I was the one who came up with the idea of using the gallery as a front. Art doesn't have to be great to be valuable. You can smuggle a lot of things under the guise of a painting."

"I bet it was challenging to juggle it all."

"Money talks. Many people in important positions can be bought. If money doesn't talk, there are other ways of getting people to do what you want."

"Is that what happened with Sharon?" Ava needed a few more minutes to keep her distracted.

"Sharon was overconfident," Elizabeth paused, then continued to pace. "She threatened me. Said she would go to the police and expose the whole operation. When it became clear that neither Tony nor Adam could get her to back off, I knew I had to handle it myself."

"That's cold," Ava said. "How did you lure her, Elizabeth?"

"It was easy," she smirked. "I told Sharon I wanted to talk. She refused to give me back the books, the receipts, the records. Thought she was smarter than me, but she changed her tune when I pulled out the gun."

"So, you shot her when she wouldn't give you what you wanted."

"She left me no choice. The rest was so easy. Move things around, change her name on a few transactions. As long as she was gone, nobody knew the truth."

"What about DiPalma? Your father? Adam? Did they know?"

"I already told you that men are simple creatures. They did as they were told. Tony was supposed to get rid of her body so nobody would find her. Clearly, he couldn't get the job done. If he didn't end up in that harbour, I would have killed him myself."

'Yeah, I can relate," Ava said as she got ready to move. "It's so hard to find good help these days."

Sirens sounded in the distance. They were getting closer. The sound was enough to distract Elizabeth. When she glanced away, she automatically lowered the gun. It was all Ava needed. She sprung up and swung the shovel into Elizabeth's midsection, sending her stumbling backwards.

The gun fell to the ground as Elizabeth charged at Ava. She was surprisingly fit and agile for her age. She swiped at Ava, her nails clawing across her face.

"Do you really think you're going to get out of here alive?" Elizabeth hissed as her boot expertly connected with Ava's knee, almost sending her on the floor.

"I'm not my mother," Ava winced as she wiped the blood off her lip.

Elizabeth snatched her hair and yanked it hard, forcing Ava's head to the side. As she looked down at her, ready to slap her again, Ava's fist shot out and connected with her jaw. As Elizabeth's grip loosened, Ava elbowed her in the stomach and followed up with another punch. This time it connected with Elizabeth's nose. She definitely wasn't a crier.

Elizabeth stumbled back and tripped over Kevin's body. She crashed to the ground like a fallen tree stump, blinking in surprise as she struggled to breathe. Their eyes connected as Ava stood over her, holding the shovel to her throat.

"Don't even try it," she warned and wiped the blood off her face.

As Elizabeth moaned in pain, Ava limped over to the pile Kevin dropped on the floor. Under the tarp, she found a bag with rope and large zip ties. She grabbed both and limped back to Elizabeth. She got one of the zip ties and secured it around Elizabeth's ankles. Deciding that securing the zip ties behind Elizabeth's back was beyond her strength, Ava straddled the woman and forced her hands together. She secured them tightly and waited for the cops to arrive.

CHAPTER 21

When Ava woke up in the hospital, she had to remind herself that it was over. Her room was filled with flowers, cards and stuffed animals from well-wishers. The sun was shining through the window, and there was soft music playing on the radio. It was a nice change from the dingy warehouse.

Her face was still swollen and bruised, but it was healing. Thankfully, her nose wasn't broken, but she wouldn't have felt anything anyway with all the pain meds she was on right now. The doctors told her that her knee would require some physiotherapy, but there were no broken bones.

She couldn't say the same thing about Elizabeth Northam. She had a broken nose, a couple of fractured ribs and a piss poor attitude. Ava didn't feel bad about putting her in a hospital after their little chat. When the police hauled her away, she threatened to have them fired and spewed very creative insults at anyone within earshot.

She looked beside her. Nick was slumped in a chair, his eyes were closed, and he looked asleep. He still had on the suit she saw him wearing in what seemed like a different lifetime.

"Am I dead?" she asked.

His eyes flew open, taking a moment to register what was happening.

"Hey," he said, surprised. "Why would you think you're dead?"

"Well, you're wearing a suit, I feel like I've been hit by a truck," she shrugged and laughed. "I used the panic button you gave me," she said in a serious tone.

"Yes," he smiled. "You did. You did good."

"I wasn't sure it worked," she told him. "He gave me something."

"It's okay," he said. "You don't have to talk about it right now."

"I want to," she said. "I'm here because you gave me that stupid button. I threw up. He must have put it in my drink, and it made me sick, so I threw up. He put me in the trunk, and I couldn't see. That's why I wasn't sure the button worked."

Nick felt something twist inside him. Her face was bruised and swollen. He saw the rope burns on her skin and the bruised knuckles before they treated her, so he knew what was under the bandages. Thinking of what she went through still made his blood boil with rage, but this wasn't the time for that.

"He clearly didn't know who he was dealing with," he smiled.

"Too bad for him," she giggled.

"Geez, what did they give you?" he smiled. "Those are some heavy-ass pain killers."

"You know," she said. "I think I'm done with Sharon now. After I finish the season about her case, I'm ready to let her go."

"That's good," he said. "Does that mean I still have a job?"

She reached out and touched his face. The drugs were making her very sleepy.

"You're so pretty," she mumbled.

"See? I knew you were getting sweet on me," he laughed. If she was making jokes, she was okay.

"You wish," she smiled. "But you can still work for me if you want. It's so hard to get good help, you know."

As she fell back asleep, Nick got up and went to find her parents. He ran into them in the hallway as they were coming back with coffee.

"She woke up," he told them. "She's loopy but seems coherent."

"Thank you again," Michael said as he handed him a cup. "For everything."

"It was nothing."

"You know it wasn't," Joan said. "Don't take it the wrong way, Nick, but you should go home and get some sleep."

"I am," he said. "My cousin is coming to get me."

Nick went home and crashed. It was a long night.

***

Several days later, they all gathered in Stan's living room. Joan made tea and coffee for everyone and kept fussing with everything to ensure everyone had enough refreshments. Keeping busy was her way of dealing with everything that happened and making sure she didn't fall apart. As long as her hands were busy, she held steady.

She glanced over at Michael, who was still on edge. They were coping together as best as they could with Ava's kidnapping and the truth about Sharon. Joan didn't doubt even for a minute that they would be okay. It would take time, she thought, and they had plenty of it to deal with processing it all.

She looked over at Ava. She was a lot stronger than any of them would have expected, and Joan was so very proud of her. It made her heart complete with love to see her daughter because that's how she always felt about Ava, finally letting go of the past. She was always too restless. Maybe this closure would help her find calm.

Joan sat down beside her husband and grasped his hand as he reached for her. They both looked over at the two detectives that came to give them an update.

"Please tell me that woman will pay for Sharon's death," Stan said. "She deserves to be behind bars for the rest of her life."

"We do have a solid case against her," Tyler told him. "Between Sharon's notes, the documents we found in DiPalma's safety deposit box and the evidence we have from her house and office, it will be hard for her to deny it all."

"We also have Ava's recording and her testimony against Elizabeth Northam," Jones added. "She might deny her involvement in Sharon's death and the money laundering, but she can't get out of killing her own son."

"I still can't believe she just shot him," Ava shrugged, the image of Kevin's body dropping in front of her still fresh in her mind. "I don't even think she thought twice about that."

"She's a killer, Ava," Tyler told her. "She's killed many people in her life when they became inconvenient. Based on what we found, DiPalma was her accomplice for a while, but she didn't hesitate to do the dirty work herself, and she did. He cleaned up after her a lot, but he seemed to have had a change of heart after their son was born. That's probably why he got a safety deposit box in a different province. He was the one with the proof of her crimes."

"Do you think he took that evidence from Sharon, or did he have it all along?" Ava asked.

"We won't know for sure. Sharon had copies. These were detailed, but what he had is more damning. That's what Elizabeth was looking for. Whether Sharon had it or not didn't matter. She knew too much, and that made her a threat."

"She told me that she offered Sharon a deal," Ava said. Stan's arm automatically wrapped around her shoulder with a reassuring squeeze. "Elizabeth tried to turn Sharon, and when that didn't work, she tried to bribe her."

"I told you that she wasn't like that," Stan said proudly. "My daughter wasn't a criminal. She was trying to do the right thing."

"She definitely was, Mr. Novak," Tyler agreed.

"What happens now?" Michael asked.

"We're still gathering evidence and piecing it all together," Jones said. "Then it goes to the courts. We'll be working closely with the Crown Attorney Office on putting together the strongest case we can. They will be taking the case against Elizabeth to court. Until then, she remains in custody."

"What about Kevin?" Ava asked. "Did he really kill his uncle?"

"We have every reason to believe that he did," Tayler and Jones exchanged a look. "The evidence recovered from his apartment leaves us little doubt that his mother was pulling the strings. He likely did what she told him. He was also the person responsible for the dry-ice bomb that blew up outside your house."

"We also found evidence that conclusively ties him to the break-in here," Jones added. "He was driving the dark sedan and the pickup truck. We are also looking at his involvement with the death of Frank Mitchell."

"That man was not interested in solving Sharon's case," Stan muttered. "I can't say I'm sorry he's dead."

"Grandpa," Ava said.

"Well, it's true," Stan crossed his arms in defiance. "He was involved in this scheme from the start."

"There is an ongoing investigation into many other individuals as well," Tyler said. "The case brought to light many people who benefited from looking the other way or took bribes. The Northams had deep pockets and used their power effectively to get what they wanted. Sharon was going to expose that."

"I'm just glad this thing is over," Ava said. "I think I need a vacation."

***

Sharon's case made headlines across the country as more details became known to the public. Ava avoided talking to the media as long as she could. While she recovered, Elizabeth Northam was stewing behind bars. There was nothing her fancy lawyers could do to get the charges against her dropped, no matter how much she berated them. It gave Ava a little sense of satisfaction to know that she wouldn't be getting her way anytime soon.

Ava finally agreed to do the press conference as her last tribute to Sharon. She would be back later to testify in court, but she was going to focus on her life until that time came. She started that with a makeover. She was tired of looking like a dead woman all the time.

Ava had cut her into a sleek, long bob. She added caramel highlights and chestnut hues and decided to let her bangs grow out. Dressed in a black pantsuit, she looked and felt like a new woman.

Ava walked up to the podium and glanced at her parents as they stood with Stan on the side. They would get their turn to speak too. In the crowd, familiar faces looked on encouragingly behind the cameras and reporters. Lori, Odessa and Steve stood with Nick as he smiled at her. Ava admitted that she liked the dressed-up-in-a-suit Nick just as much as she did the jeans-and-t-shirt Nick. He was, after all, an excellent assistant no matter how he looked.

She cleared her throat and adjusted the mic. A hush fell over the crowd.

"Sharon Novak was a beloved daughter and a devoted mother," she began. "She was also a staunch believer in truth and doing the right thing.

"For the last twenty-five years, her memory had been besmirched by those that ruthlessly killed her to protect their own greed. Sharon did not steal any money. She did not abandon her daughter, and she didn't run off. She died because someone else decided that she was inconvenient and knew too much."

Ava paused as she looked over the crowd and continued.

"The people who killed Sharon didn't just take away my mother. They robbed both of us of the experience only a mother and daughter can share. She will never see me grow up, get married or have kids. I will never know what she was like other than what I'm told by those that knew her."

Ava could see her grandfather wiping away tears and her father's comforting grip on his shoulder. Sharon wasn't here in person, but she was always here in spirit.

"My own memories of her have slipped away with time," she said in a steady voice. "And while today I don't even know the woman that was my mother, I see her every time I look in the mirror. That's my special connection to Sharon that nobody can take away from me. It is through me that she lives on."

Ava thanked Detective Burnett for his unwavering commitment to solving her mother's case and those that worked tirelessly to find her.

Later, when it was all done, she decided it was time for a new chapter in her life. She looked up as Nick, Lori, Odessa, and Lori came up to her. They were her friends, and that made her happy.

"Ready to go?" Nick asked.

"Yeah," she said. "Let's get out of here."

ABOUT AUTHOR

Kasia Chojecki is an author, blogger and freelance writer based in Toronto, Canada.

Before becoming a writer, Kasia had worked for over ten years in economic development where she worked with start-ups and existing businesses in Canada and abroad. She assisted many of them with business development, funding and business planning.

When she's not travelling, Kasia brings to life many of the stores that live in her imagination. She also loves to travel, discover new places and write about them. As an avid reader, Kasia loved a good mystery with a dash of adventure.

Kasia holds a Bachelor's Degree in History from the University of Toronto and a post-grad Certificate in Communications from Centennial College.

Kasiawrites Cultural Travel Blog

Adventure, exploration and discovery with a focus on responsible travel. An exciting way of learning about the world as well as self-reflection and personal freedom. A place for curious travellers, looking for new experiences, discovering new things and learning something new along the way.

https://kasiawrites.com

Amongst Romans Italy Travel

Everything Italy from and outsider's perspective. For the love of all things Italian. Italy travel tips, guides and inspiration.

https://amongstromans.com

The Blogging Game

Practical advice on how to turn your blog into a business.

(Available on Amazon and iTunes)

Printed in Great Britain
by Amazon

67916124R10183